The House of S: Catherine's Story

By Elizabeth Fowler

To my Mas, who forever keeps me hungering for more.

Two chips in a cup. A simple dichotomy. One inscribed with the word pleasure. The other, pain. My choice -- to reach in, to select one, to step into an unknown space, one that is both physical and ethereal.

I swallow, my mouth dry. S looks unflappable, as though time spent waiting is as valuable as time spent doing. I sense that she will not remove the weight of this decision, not even bear a tiny bit of it. This is 100% on me.

I uncross my legs and sit upright. I notice the cushions are unbelievably soft. How did I miss that detail? The chandelier, an elegant one perfectly proportioned for the space, is casting just enough light for me to see her skin. It's milky white with the finest of wrinkles at the edges of her eyes. She seems eternal, like some great monument in a past civilization that stands to this day.

With an audible "all right then" escaping from my throat -- a pep talk of sorts --, I slowly, hesitantly, reach into the cup. I feel exactly two cold chips. It's like a high stakes game of poker in a backroom in Vegas where the gambler has wagered it all. My fingers select the bottom chip as though it's an elusive prize. With a small measure of determination, I pull it out and put it in her perfectly manicured hand. My heart beating against my chest wall, I lean in just a bit as she reveals my choice…

My choice is...pain.

S raises her eyes to read mine. The corner of her mouth relaxes into not quite a smile. She states in the most immoveable tone, "Perfect. Well done."

I realize I've given you no context for this. I've jumped into the journey with none of the back story. And certainly, there is no way to make sense of this without understanding what brought me to this place.

My name is Catherine Standish Bolton. I have been described as a forty-something mover and shaker. I have fought and scraped, traded and compromised my way to the top. The employees at Bolton Financial - all 2,500 some of them - see me as a cross between an ice princess and the ruthless queen mother. Finance is a man's world even today. As a woman, I've made every sacrifice possible to build this company, and no one, not even myself, will I let get in the way.

My days are tension-filled tests where countless decisions determine success or failure, stock price gain or loss. My dreams are filled with balance sheets and profit and loss statements, annual reports, and press conferences. I am a master of my domain but it has come at a cost.

I think it was my fortieth birthday when I began to wake up. That milestone was marked with a 14-hour workday that concluded with a nip of single malt with my CFO. My office was filled with bouquets from sycophants hoping to draw my favor, a sickly-sweet smell of Stargazer lilies mixing with tuberose and freesia.

As I lay my head on my perfectly made bed in my perfectly arranged and managed apartment, I thought how imperfect, fucked, really, my life was. Where was the living? Was the sum total of my being a collection of mergers and acquisitions, IPOs, and short sales? It was then that I decided to find a life coach. I mean, I had a trainer for working out, a stylist for my appearance and wardrobe, an interior designer for my apartment and Bolton Financial's offices. I had a chef, a gardener, a driver, a pilot, a physiotherapist, an IT person. Fuck, I had someone who specialized in supporting every aspect of my life, except, that is, the part that had to do with living.

So that's when I determined to turn things around, under the care of an expert, someone who would guide me back to living and not just having the trappings of a life.

Brad seemed reasonable enough. He had worked for the best. Everyone just raved about how much clarity he brought to their thinking. I was pleasantly surprised at how at ease I felt in my first session. My usual guardedness slipped away. I didn't even feel embarrassed describing a demeaning situation at Harvard Business School where a male peer sabotaged my presentation with remorseless glee.

Brad seemed content to let me guide the conversation. He would pause and ask questions, nod, scribble, empathize. It was like a confessional where there was no guilt, simply one's story. And I had no idea how much I needed to tell my story.

Each session felt cathartic. But still, I was stuck, stuck doing what I had done so well for 18 years. Hmmm.

Six months into these weekly sessions (at $300 a pop, mind you), I paused and said, "I think that's it. I think that's my story."

"And is this how your story ends, Catherine?"

I was stunned, speechless actually. Shit. I mean, yeah, isn't that why I was here, so my story WOULDN'T end like this?

"I was hoping you could help me find a way out. I mean, not a way out of my business, but a way out of my rut. You know, a way back to some kind of newness, discovery."

"I have been waiting for you to ask this question," Brad said in rather measured tones. "No one moves from without. It always comes from within. One has to want it badly enough. I think you perhaps want it badly enough. Do you, do you want it badly enough?"

The illusive IT. What was IT that I wanted? That's what HE was supposed to help me figure out. I felt no further along than when I started.

"Catherine, sometimes we know what we don't want and defining what we do want is hard. You have shared about all the ways you have mastered your world, and yet, you feel something is lacking. You are, by all external measures, at the top of your game, and yet, here we are. So, let me ask you again, Catherine. Do you want it badly enough?"

I feel at this moment about five-years-old. Some adult in my life is asking me a simple question, and yet, I cannot answer. I simply don't know what IT is, so how can I know if I want IT badly enough.

Brad senses my deflation. After a long deep breath, he says, "Catherine, you only know half of yourself, that part that takes on every obstacle as a challenge to be conquered. You have walled off the part that hungers to be vulnerable and open. I am not even sure you know what I mean when I say that. That's the cost you've paid in building Bolton Financial, independently, fearlessly, single-mindedly. That is why you are here, is it not?"

With an uncharacteristic quiver in my lip, I nod my head. Yup. I have become an efficient machine of my own making. I hunger for my humanity to come back.

"I have an idea, a rather unusual one. That's why I keep asking you if you want it badly enough. If you say yes to my proposal, you will be choosing a journey where you willingly give up a huge measure of control. I think this will be, wait, I know this will be very hard for you. Not impossible, but totally against the grain. You dominate your world, and to know yourself, you will need to find yourself on the other side of that coin. You will need to cede control. So let me ask you again, do you want it badly enough?"

Shit... fuck... damn... really? Have you ever hungered for something desperately and yet feared it in equal measure? This is where I sat in that moment, caught between a desperate if undefined longing and sheer terror. Yet, I hear myself responding, like some alien inside is speaking, "Yes, absolutely. I want it badly enough," and that simple sentence brought me to S.

I had no idea such places existed. I mean, I had heard of BDSM, generally as silly off-color references at cocktail parties. But this, this was the real thing.

S was in her element. I am generally unflappable - one doesn't build a multi-billion-dollar company and get disarmed easily - but I couldn't believe how I felt in her presence. It was immediate, too. It's like she read me like a book and nothing I could do would hide any of my secrets.

Brad had explained that S would at once build me up and tear me down, and in the process, I would somehow find myself, or at least, discover that part that was missing. It would be a rebirth through fire, a phoenix rising from ashes.

The first visit was uneventful, a chance for S to get to know me and for me to specify limits. She presented me with an intake form that detailed countless possibilities. She was very clear: I was only to mark "no go" on items I truly, under no circumstance, would consider. She said that it was ALWAYS my choice, but too many limits would hamper her ability to serve me as she hoped to.

We were seated in that same comfortable room with facing couches covered in the most luxurious soft pillows. Heavy drapes framed tall windows. Layers of sheer fabric -- Roman shades -- kept the light soft even during the day. The space was a silk cocoon out of which a butterfly might emerge, but only after the caterpillar dissolves and is remade completely.

Serve me? That gave me pause. "What would that look like?" I asked.

"I will design a sequence of experiences tailored just for you," S replied. "You will accept the path and do your best to meet each task or challenge. It won't be easy. You are so one-sided. You know nothing of the dream-state that is submission, so you will likely push back to a point. It will be up to you where this goes and how fast you get there."

I swallow. How badly do I want IT? How badly do I want to live again? I smile and say, "That sounds comforting and disarming at the same time. I have never backed down from a challenge, so I am all in." Was that me or my ego committing? Fuck.

S leaves me with a glass of champagne and a four-page checklist, again admonishing me to be very judicious about what I nix. Oh, and she says there will be one more stop today - the wardrobe room.

So, wax play? Okay. How bad can that be?
Spanking, like a playful spanking? Sure.
Nipple clamps. Hmmm. I have no idea. Fuck.

I nixed choking, blood and scat play. I marked other items as maybes - some of the bondage types seemed, well, extreme. And the humiliation/degradation list? Holy fuck. What was I doing?

Checklist complete, an attractive female in the most seductive attire ushered me to the wardrobe room. As I walked behind her, I couldn't take my eyes off her perfectly sculpted backside, framed in a teddy/thong of sorts. Her ass was lusciously round and muscular, clearly the product of endless squats and lunges, her skin was a milk-coffee shade, and from what I could tell, flawless. The blood began to flow between my legs. My clit swelled. Shit. It took everything in me not to reach out and cup her cheeks.

I had been backstage in New York to see where costumers do their work, but nothing prepared me for this space. Row upon row of the sexiest clothing I had ever seen. My escort showed me to a dressing room where pre-selected items hung. She insisted on staying with me, assisting with sizing, and adjustment of straps. And, oh my god, there were straps!

The first item was a luscious kimono. She said I would enter and exit each time wrapped in this kimono. It was navy blue with turquoise, pink, and red. Birds and flowers exuberantly covered every inch. It was a dream.

Then came four outfits, each more "exposed" than the prior ones. The first was a teddy thong like she was wearing. The breasts however were fully exposed. The teddy managed to still lift and support each tit but more like a shelf for them to be displayed for all.

The second was a cloth wrap reminiscent of that Jane Fonda classic, Barbarella. It covered one butt cheek only and wound its way upward, covering only one breast and shoulder.

The third was simpler still -- a skinny waist belt with a sheer triangle of fabric in the front and thong in back. And nothing for the top.

The fourth -- this one made my heart skip a beat -- the fourth was a harness. That was it, a leather harness and throat collar. Fuck. What have I done?

The date for my first scene was set for Saturday. As my work week wore on, I, the laser-focused ice maiden, struggled endlessly to keep it together. Aside from the wild wonderings of my mind, there was the challenge of keeping this "therapy" a secret. I would, for the time being, have to face this completely alone.

Saturday morning came, and I panicked. S must have had clients with cold feet before, because at 9 am, my doorbell rang and Alice, my house manager, brought in a gorgeous bouquet and a handwritten note:

Catherine,

Excitement and fear are the same emotion just viewed from a different perspective. Surely, you are feeling one, or the other, or both. Know that whatever is planned will show you parts of yourself you long to know.

- S

Her signature was the most elegant curvy S I had ever seen. It seemed to embody her being - larger than life, something of the ages.

I changed clothes at least six times, finally settling on a sleeveless dress and heels, something classy yet sexy. I thought how humorous this exercise in dressing was...a lamb to the slaughter dressed in heels. Oh, well. Fuck me.

My driver dropped me at the House of S. The outside looked like every other brownstone on the block, well-kept, with the secrets of the place concealed behind blinds and drapes. No one would have suspected a thing.

I am greeted at the door by a uniformed doorman, who escorts me to the same room I left a week ago. A carafe of water and a glass of champagne, freshly poured, await. I choose the champagne.

The time passes at what feels like a ridiculously slow pace. My palms are sweating now. I feel rocky and uncertain, like the feeling one gets looking over a ledge from 85 stories high in the air.

I am startled by the door. Expecting S, I am unnerved when the same assistant who helped me with the wardrobe appears. She tells me to bring the champagne and follow her. Instead of the large costume room, she takes me upstairs to a small dressing room, outfitted in a period-fashion, almost Victorian, though understated. Opulent cushioned surfaces in burgundy and gold match heavy drapery and thick rugs. The wood floor appears original and creaks a bit as I walk to the dressing table. The assistant tells me that today's outfit will consist of the sheer fabric thong and the harness. She explains I may need assistance in maintaining my position during the session, and the harness will help. My mind races. What the fuck does that mean?

I gulp the champagne, hoping to calm my nerves. The assistant begins to take my clothes off and hang them up on satin covered hangers. She offers the washroom and strongly encourages me to empty my bladder as "It may be a while…" What have I done?

She returns to fix my hair in a high ponytail, secured with a ribbon. She tightens the harness so as it moves, so will I. She has me stand so I can put the kimono on. It feels better to be covered. She looks me over from top to bottom and says, approvingly, "There we are. You look perfect." And with that, we leave the safety of the dressing room.

She leads me Into a small elevator and presses the basement button. As the door closes, I realize she is leaving me at this point. I am on my own now.

Two floors down and the doors open. Waiting for me with a look I cannot begin to describe is a gorgeous man. He is muscular, tall, and smooth, with flawless skin. He is at once dispassionate and desirous. I sense a level of self-control I envy. He clips a leash to my collar and begins walking. I am so taken aback, I don't move right away. I stumble out, and he issues this warning, "You will follow or there will be a consequence. Do you understand, Catherine? It's up to you how hard this will be. I assure you, you will bend. Sooner or later, you will bend."

I pick up the pace and attempt to walk next to him. BIG mistake. He stops, turns, and smacks me across the face. The shock of it all delays the sensation of pain. I am certain I look like a wild animal, cornered in a hunt.

"Catherine, you are under my control. Is that clear?" I nod. If it wasn't clear a minute ago, it is now.

"Catherine, you will not walk in front nor beside me. If I ask you to crawl, you will crawl. Do you understand?" My head bobs. My heart is pounding. I am terrified.

"Whatever I do, it is for you. I am committed to you. That will not look like all those people in your world who step out of your way. Still, I am committed. And if you do your part, I will become devoted even, though not a form of devotion you are used to. Whatever correction you need, I will deliver it swiftly."

I nod my head. He responds, "I don't hear you. What's that?"

"Yes."

"Yes, who?"

"Yes…" I am unsure what to say. My mistake is met with a slap on the other cheek, hard enough my eyes tear up."

"Yes, sir. That's how you answer, Catherine. Yes, sir. Do you understand?"

"Yes, sir." My head bows instinctively. I lower my eyes, and we begin to walk again. I have lost my usual confidence completely, an alien in a new world.

The room is so dark I am unsure of its dimensions. Under a dim light from an exposed bulb hanging in an industrial cage like those seen on construction sites is a wooden structure with rings, ropes, and cuffs. My trainer (that's how I think of him at this moment) attaches my leash to a ring and then sets about affixing cuffs to my wrists and ankles. These he connects to the wooden supports. He shortened the ropes so that my legs are apart and my arms are spread. I am helpless and open.

It's then that I notice the table. It must have been there the whole time, but it only became visible once my eyes adjusted to the low light. My heart goes into my throat. There, laid out in organized and methodical fashion, are every manner and type of whip and paddle. The trainer walks over and selects a riding crop and tests it on his hand. The sound sends terror up my back. My skin is a mass of goosebumps. He walks over and begins to rub the riding crop along the outline of my body, from my bound wrists to my ankles, up the inside of my thigh, stopping at my crotch. He pulls back ever so slightly and delivers a strike to my buttocks just outside my anus. This is followed immediately by a stinging blow to my clit. I swear there is no air in my lungs. I am gasping to pull it in. The sensation is not like anything I have ever felt. Yes, it was painful, but it was also intensely pleasurable. How can that be? He moves on.

Next, he selects a cat-o-nine-tails. He teases my back and buttocks and then begins to methodically deliver blows. He stays in one place until the sensation shifts from pain to a kind of euphoric numbness, like the nerves can no longer register pain. I feel my skin heating up and sweat beads on my forehead. He finishes with a long whip with a small tip that bites into my flesh. I feel welts emerging. Because he only strikes the areas he has warmed up, I am somehow able to withstand each blow without tears.

He pauses to unclip me and I think to myself, "That was manageable." Only then do I realize he is fixing me to the structure again, this time my front facing outward. He works over my stomach and breasts. He continues to strike my clit, delivering repeated intense waves of sensation, until I nearly lose my footing. My head droops. Sweat pours down my face.

He starts on my thighs, paying particular attention to my inner thigh, especially the tender upper part. I raise my head enough to look at him. I want to see his face. He meets my insolence with a slap, and I drop my head again.

When I am certain I can take no more, he moves me to a bench where he again binds me so movement is nominal. My feet hang over the edge. Relentless he hits the bottom of my feet with paddles, sending waves of pain, followed by euphoria, over and over.

After some time, he stops. Carefully, he puts his tools away. He fetches my kimono and unclips me. He helps me slip my arms in and he ties the belt carefully around my waist. I am trembling. He picks me up, my head laying against his shoulder. He carries me to an adjacent room. Gently, he sits me in a soft overstuffed chair and places my legs on an ottoman. He rings a bell, and momentarily someone shuffles in with tea. The trainer sits beside me and raises the cup to my lips. He stops, sets the cup down, and instead raises my chin. His grasp is firm but caring now. My eyes look into his. He says, "You did well, my pet. You did very well. Let me reward you now."

The next hour is a dream filled with tea, bits of chocolate, and a bubble bath. The same man who inflicted blows is gently washing my body, caressing and kissing my welts. He cocoons me in an oversized towel and lays me down on a bed laden with down-filled duvets. He lies beside me, holding me, whispering my name, telling me he is pleased with my devotion. I drift off.

Sometime later, the assistant from this morning gently wakes me, and takes me back to change. I struggle to fit my swollen feet into the heels. I survey the damage and it is surprisingly minimal. My skin looks mildly sunburned.

When I reach my apartment, I realize I am starving. It's already 8 pm and I left for the House of S at 10 this morning. My house manager greets me with a tray of beverage options - water, white wine, orange juice, and tea. Dinner is plated and in the oven, waiting, she says. Would I like to eat? OMG, yes. I restrain myself and tell her yes in a much more controlled tone than the child that is inside me who is screaming for food. She directs me to a bag on the table, tied with a creamy white ribbon. A calling card with that same elegant S is attached. Hmm. What has she left for me now?

Inside is a note, written in her lovely hand:

Catherine,

Congratulations on beginning your journey today. I know your mind is swirling with thoughts. Let these flow by. Watch them as they enter and allow them to leave. Then, examine what's left in that space where there is only now.

Consider how it felt today. There were moments of pain, of pleasure, and of relief. Were you anywhere but simply here, here in each and every moment?

On more practical matters, the bag contains a jar of arnica cream and arnica tablets. For the next 24 hours, no alcohol. [Damn. That white wine looked luscious.] *Drink lots of water. Slather your body in the arnica cream. Follow the directions for the tablets. You will recover remarkably quickly if you follow these steps. Oh, and no alarm clock for tomorrow morning. Sleep until you wake.*

S

My house manager brings dinner on a tray. I devour every bite. Somehow everything tasted more delicious, more real than I remember food ever tasting. I drag myself upstairs and post-arnica treatment, crawl into my perfectly made bed.

My next visit to the House of S is a check-in with S herself. S shares that she prides herself on knowing her clients very well. It's in knowing her clients that she can craft a meaningful journey. She uses that word all the time...journey, like there's a starting point and some end-goal in mind. The challenge is that S is the only one who knows the end goal. The client steps off the metaphorical cliff into a vast unknown, trusting in her expertise.

S is again wearing something unusual. It's like she has a wardrobe made from pieces from countless Hollywood movies. Today, she appears Asian, in close-fitting silk pants and a long top slit up the sides. The tones are pink and purple - bright, regal, loud. Yet, somehow she looks perfect in this in her brownstone domain.

Instead of the room with facing couches, we are in her office itself. There's a massive desk that speaks of power and wealth. She directs me, however, to a pair of overstuffed chairs facing each other at an intimate distance. A small tall table holds a fresh flower arrangement. The tendrils of honeysuckle scent the air. Small side tables hold nibbles -- sugar coated almonds, seeded crackers smeared with scallion cream cheese and topped with half a cherry tomato, a swirl of apple and pear slices punctuated with plump fresh blueberries. Instead of champagne, S has offered a rare port, something much more substantive.

S begins, "Catherine, what are your thoughts about your first scene?"

Honestly? Where to begin… "I have to say I had no idea what to expect and I am not even sure it actually happened. It was like a dream, both one I want to dream again and one I never want to dream again."

"Ah...good. You are struggling a bit. To be expected. Years of conditioning to be the one on top in your world make it hard for you to experience the flip side. Don't worry, you will absolutely get there, Catherine. This, I am certain."

I crunch into an almond, the sugar crust rubbing against my tongue. "And where is there, S?"

"That is the question, isn't it? Are you feeling that you don't yet know?"

I take a sip of port and think I must add this to my wine cellar. It is yummy. "S, where do I go from here? I mean, that first event, well, I can't imagine topping that." OMG, had I just thrown down the gauntlet? Shit.

"Don't concern yourself with what's next. Let me, let us, relieve you of the burden of planning or orchestrating. I look forward to hearing your thoughts after next Saturday." And with that, our conversation came to a close.

Saturday arrives and I am again in a twitter about what to wear. I tell myself, *this is bullshit*. I mean my clothes take me there and bring me home. That's it. I finally settle on mom jeans, a loose sweatshirt, and Birkenstocks.

My driver raises one eyebrow slightly when he sees my unconventional attire. I realize he may never have seen me dressed like this. On the drive I find myself hoping I will have the same trainer. I don't even know his name.

The doorman swings the heavy ornate door open and once again I step into the House of S. There's a slight spring in my step this time, less foreboding, more on the edge of excitement. Hmm. Curious.

The same assistant greets me and takes me to the dressing room. She shares that my "master" has requested a different outfit, so she presents me with a black lace corset. My breasts sit on ledges of cups perfectly matched to my size, nipples perched like contented birds on a wire. A matching thong is window dressing -- the corset raises up and frames each butt cheek. I feel like a complete harlot and it feels delicious.

Again, the assistant states that my "master" selected this outfit. My heart skips a beat. Did he? Did he really? My labia begin to swell as a tickle of desire builds at the thought of him choosing this piece.

She adds one final touch, a black lace collar, complete with a skinny black leather leash. I feel the pride of the pet, like a poodle returning home from a day of grooming, awaiting the complements of the master. Oh my.

He comes to the door and simply takes me in with his eyes. I feel myself blushing, my head and gaze instinctively lower. He makes a gesture for me to turn around. Slowly, delightfully, I turn. I hear a low sound from his throat when I present my backside. As I finish turning, I realize he is now right next to me, just inches away. I can barely stand the tension of his closeness. He takes my chin in his hand, and lifts my face up. He looks straight into my eyes and says, "Catherine, you are luscious. You are my perfect pet. I am most pleased."

I draw my eyes downward, blushing even more, but he is relentless. He again makes me meet his gaze, "You are a prize worth owning, and I will own you, Catherine. I will."

With that pronouncement, the assistant hands over the leash and we begin the walk, me dutifully two steps behind.

As he is again adding cuffs and attaching me to the wooden frame, I find the courage to speak: "What is your name?"

"What is your name, sir. Surely, you want to start our time together off right, don't you? Why would you spoil it with insolent behavior, Catherine?"

"Oh, sir. I am so sorry. I am just, I am just, wow, how do I put it? I am just so drawn to you, sir, so drawn to you."

"Of course you are, Catherine. You are mine. Don't you realize this? And, as to my name, you may call me sir or master. Perhaps one day, when you have proven yourself, when I fully sense your devotion, I will tell you my name."

The corset prevented my master from hitting my back or stomach directly. This made him focus in on more tender parts, like my buttocks and breasts, which soon shone red from the attention of small whips and crops. He had a technique of pulling back each hit so the effect was a sting more than a blow. The sensation was like being stung by a wasp, but as the strikes multiplied, the stinging became numbness, which, in turn, became release. I felt drugged.

My thighs received extra attention as did my cheeks. He would lift my chin and slap me. In those moments, I feared him, but the fear was an aphrodisiac. My vagina grew wetter with each strike. He took note of this as juices began to run down my thighs.

"Ah, warming up, are we? Very good. Very, very good. My pet, you are doing so well. I am most pleased."

For whatever reason, he spared my clit. I found myself longing for him to strike me there, and yet, he did not.

And unlike last time, he returned again and again to my front and backside, as sensations subsided, he doubled-down his attack. I felt myself growing woozy. My knees buckled to the point where the wrist cuffs were my only support. He sensed I was at the end of what I could tolerate. Again, he wrapped me in the kimono and carried me to the next room to rest and recover, or so I thought.

Instead, he laid me down on a narrow bed covered with silk quilts. He spread my legs and buried his head between them. Oh, fuck. He zeroed in on my clit, sucking it in between his teeth and massaging it back and forth. I had never felt anything like this before. Shit.

He paused and turned me over, raising my buttocks in the air, and placing pillows underneath me. He spread my cheeks and began to lick from the back edge of my vagina to my ass. He circled my ass again and again with his tongue. I heard an animal moaning and realized it was me. I was the animal. He pressed in now, tongue against ass. The juices ran from my vagina like a stream. He flipped me back over and again sucked my clit, now a sphere of ridiculous proportion, into his mouth, and rubbed his tongue against it, as the moaning sounds grew from deep inside me. Every time I got close to cumming, he slowed the pace. Finally, after what seemed like hours, I came, over and over and over for minutes of bliss. I cried out to God, to Jesus. I said, "Oh fuck, oh fuck, oh fuck," until my legs turned to jello and my body quivered in one last final climax.

He lay next to me, stroking my hair and face, I could feel his breath on my ear. His body spooned mine. Then he whispered in my ear, "My name is Adam," and I swear, I came again.

Adam continued his aftercare by slipping me into a warm tub. I was not allowed to wash myself. This he did with the utmost care. He used a soft sponge to slide over every inch. Between my legs, however, he used only his hand. He had let the water begin to drain out and when there were just a few inches of water remaining, he closed the drain and restarted the tap in a slow, steady flow. He selected a special soap from the adjacent table and drizzled it over my crotch. He worked it into a gentle lather and then moved his powerful hand back and forth and up and down, each stroke building in intensity. He turned his hand so his thumb was inside, closest to my body. As he moved from ass to vagina to clit, he allowed his thumb to follow the contours precisely, teasingly. My legs relaxed completely. I slid back so my head was in the water. Adam washed and stroked, the slippery soap bubbles the perfect lubricant, until I came. Again, he sustained the sensation in a way no one had ever done.

When I simply couldn't cum any longer, Adam used a ladle to pour clean, warm water over my crotch. He carefully spread my labia to assure the rinse water reached all the essential places. I felt like a toddler in the hands of my mother, awakening, perhaps for the first time, to this special erogenous zone.

He lifted me from the tub and carried me to the bed, laying me down on fluffy towels. He patted me dry, careful not to rub the skin that had endured so much already. He massaged arnica cream all over, working with small gentle strokes. He then covered me with a cotton sheet and a duvet, and lay down beside me to stroke my head. It was only moments before I was asleep.

God knows how much time passed, but when I woke, it was dark outside. The female assistant was sitting nearby, my mom jeans, sweatshirt, and Birkenstocks in hand. I blushed at the thought of how long she had been there with me sleeping like a baby.

My driver was at the ready to take me home. He never asked questions and was accustomed to the idea of sticking with his task and not prying into circumstances. (IPO's and short sales require a level of confidentiality and secrecy, and any indiscretion on his part would have cost him his job years back.)

At home, my assistant was at the ready, this time only orange juice, water, and weak tea as beverages. And once again, I ate every piece of food on the plate as though I hadn't eaten in weeks. S had sent over a note and a small bouquet of honeysuckle and gardenia.

Catherine,

My, my, such progress you are making. I have never heard of Adam sharing his name this soon. He is truly growing in his devotion to you. I am sure you feel that in many ways. You can always trust what's between your legs to let you know what is real and what is contrived.

Remember, no alcohol, lots of water, and take the arnica. Oh, and I hope you enjoy the bouquet. I noticed how much you appreciated mine. I am learning that scent matters to you so I chose only flowers with fragrance.

See you on Tuesday for your check-in.

S

I carried the bouquet upstairs and put it on my bedside table. I wanted to sleep while drinking in that sweet smell. I closed my eyes and was transported back to this afternoon. I could feel Adam's breath on my neck: "My name is Adam," I heard him whisper in his rich voice. And with that, I fell into a deep sleep.

I arrived at Tuesday's check-in straight from a high-powered meeting about a potential IPO that had some last-minute issues. S must have sensed the tension I still carried from that meeting. She called an assistant, a house masseur, to come and rub my feet and legs, neck and shoulders while we talked. I felt the stress of the day melt away.

S served a chilled Sauvignon Blanc with savory cheeses and fruit. I was coming to appreciate how thoughtful she was in all things. Truly, she was a master of this domain.

"So, Catherine, how are you feeling? Anything coming up for you?"

I really want to appear calm and collected, my usual confident and in control self. Instead, I find myself pouring out words without regard for content. "Oh, S, I don't really know where to begin. Last Saturday was the most amazing day of my life. I have never had someone so close and intimate without emotional entanglement. Don't misunderstand me. For reasons I cannot explain, I am completely under Adam's spell. I melt to his touch. I want to please him so. I want to live in that space with him where the world dissolves and it is just us."

"What do you think makes up that space?"

I have not considered this. I pause to ponder the question: *What makes up that sacred space I experienced?* "I know a big part of this is my complete vulnerability and trust. I mean, my God, I am tied to a stock of sorts. I couldn't leave without assistance, and yet, I am somehow sensing love in that restriction. Does that even make sense?"

"Yes, Catherine, it does. You are coming to know that Adam, while dominating you, is, in fact, serving you at the highest levels. His choice of whip or crop, the location, number, and depth of strikes, the pauses in between, these are all out of consideration for what you need. What will keep you present, in your body, in a moment in time."

"S, I drew the pain chip from the cup. There were two chips, pain and pleasure. Last weekend ended with the most intense pleasure I have ever experienced. But I didn't draw the pleasure chip…"

"Catherine, plain and pleasure are two sides of the same coin. You are beginning to experience pleasure in pain, are you not? Think about the fractions of a second between strikes, doesn't your body tingle? Don't you feel a rush of relief?"

More than that. I feel each strike is scratching a never-ending itch that comes from deep inside. Where does that itch, that desire come from?

"Catherine, I cannot give you your answers. I can give you experiences that help you find your answers." With that, S uncrossed her ankles and sat up, an indication that our check-in was concluding. Every time I have met with S, I feel I know more and I know less at the same time.

Saturday morning arrives, and I bound out of bed. I feel more energy and excitement than I have in decades. I spend no time selecting clothes. I grab my favorite sweat pants and t-shirt and my tried-and-true Birkenstocks. The time seems to drag on. Finally, finally, 9:30 arrives and I am once again off to the House of S.

I am tempted to push past the doorman, but I manage to rein in my impulse and act nonchalant as he swings open the heavy door. Inside, the female assistant ushers me to a dressing room. I anxiously await what I am to wear but she only offers the kimono. I cock my head to one side, "Only this?"

"Yes, ma'am. Only this."

Hmmm. Butt naked with the soft silk wrapped around me, I sit on a chair, arms crossed and wait. And wait. And wait. Finally, the door opens. Adam walks in with his usual expression, a mix of satisfaction and entitlement. I straighten up my back. My chin drops. I feel blood rushing to my cheeks. He thanks the assistant, who quietly steps out of the room. Adam speaks up, "I am not collaring you because I think you know what's expected and will comply, will you not?" I nod like a nervous schoolgirl. "Stand up then." I rise and follow him out of the room, keeping two steps behind. We don't turn to enter the usual room. Instead, we go down a hallway to the right. Adam opens a door and motions for me to step in. He follows, closes the door, and locks it. The sound of the bolt moving into place sends goosebumps up my spine.

"Take off your kimono and place it on that chair."

"Yes, sir."

"Ah, my girl has found her voice. Good. Now, come back and kneel on this cushion."

I do as instructed and find my face level with his cock. "Remove my pants." Pants isn't exactly what I would call what he is wearing. It's more than a G-string, like tight briefs cut up high on his legs and partially exposing his buttocks. My hands brush against smooth skin over taut muscles. I am dying.

I fold his pants and place them next to me. I turn back and there, full frontal, is his cock. It is partially erect, rising up to meet my mouth. Adam grabs my head and hair and pulls me in. I reach up with my hands. "Tisk, tisk, no, my girl. No hands. Mouth only." He is firm, not rough, but it's clear who is in control. His cock quickly fills with blood and extends straight out and slightly up. He adjusts the angle of my head so that my throat is further back. He explores the depths of my mouth, somehow aware of just how far he can go without making me gag.

He pulls out and tells me to lick his balls. I begin gingerly but soon find one of them flat against my mouth where I gently suck it in and out. He controls the tempo moving back into my mouth. He pulls out again and slaps my cheek with his cock. He rubs it all over my face.

Back into my mouth with more force and intensity, he is neither gentle nor brutal. I want to make him cum. I want to bring him pleasure. I want him to not be able to resist. I push myself forward to take in more. I find a way to drop my chin to lengthen my mouth further. I challenge myself to take in his entire length. While I don't completely succeed, it is enough to push him over the edge. Instead of cumming in my mouth, he pulls out and sprays cum on my face, hair and chest.

"Look at me," he says. He wipes cum from my cheek and feeds it to me. "How is that, my pet? You are so privileged to taste my cum." He scoops up more, but reserves it in his hand. He tells me to get on all fours.

He smears the cum on my ass and begins to slide a finger in and out, pushing more and more cum inside my asshole. Now two fingers, sliding in and out with his smooth cum. My vagina is ridiculously wet and begging for attention, but it is my ass he is focused on. Out of nowhere, he pulls out a toy, a long glass dildo with a large smooth head, studded with glass beads around the shaft. He wipes it against the cum on my chest and then rolls it in circles pressing gently against my anus. Like Aladin to the Cave of Wonders, this is the magic word. I open up and he slides the dildo in and out, each studded bead causing me to gasp and shake. He reaches around to my clit and massages it in circles. I hear animal moans and realize these are coming from me. He persists as I climax, sustaining the orgasm with skill I didn't know was possible.

I find myself in a ball on the floor. A mess, an ecstatic mess. He joins me, placing my head in his crotch. He tells me to take his cock again into my mouth like a baby takes a tit. When I am slow to respond, he slaps my cheek, the sting focusing my attention. In short order he has another massive erection. He slips on a condom and I am relieved we will finally have intercourse. My vagina has been aching for attention.

Instead, he hauls me over to the bed. On a small table is a bowl of oil. From the smell I can tell it's coconut oil. He instructs me to slather it on the condom and then to get on all fours. He presses the head of his penis on my ass, using the same small circular motion of the dildo to relax the muscles. I gasp when he pushes the head of his penis inside, but he waits for a moment for my body to relax again before he begins to slowly move in and out. To my astonishment, this feels heavenly. I long for him to go deeper and deeper, and as he does, I find my hand touching my clit, with the same motions he has shown me. I rise to one climax after another. He slaps my ass and then fucks me more. He goes slow as I beg for him to fuck me hard, and then he moves with the abandon of a teenager, and I cum for what seems like minutes. He pulls out, rips the condom off, and turns me over. He lets me have free reign this time and he cums into my mouth, a heavenly salty primordial soup. I love that I know what he tastes like.

He pulls me by the hair to a washbasin. He instructs me in firm tones to wash his cock and balls. I am surprised how delightful this is. I find my hand sliding between his legs and stroking the perineum. He looks down, his head cocked to one side, an eyebrow raised. Have I found a button of his? God knows, he has found all of mine.

After I finish washing him, he turns me around and tells me to spread my legs. He washes me thoroughly, sliding fingers and knuckles against my vagina and anus. I am again so aroused from his touch.

He takes me again by the hair and whispers into my ear, "I think my girl needs a spanking." The words speak to my cunt and the juices flow. Over to a chair he pulls me, turning me over his knee, he uses his hand to raise color across my ass. First, I feel pain, then the rising numbness, then the itch that begs to be scratched. My cunt is now dripping. He dips a finger in, and a soft moan leaves my lips.

"Ah, my girl is horny. You will have to work for it, my little whore." He drags me to the bed, where again he directs my head to his cock, rising up to meet my mouth. I find myself embolden and eager. I expose the head with each downward motion and attempt to slide the foreskin over it with my hand and mouth with each upward stroke. Soon, it is simply too erect to do either. He hands me a condom. I realize I have never put one on a man before. I fumble a bit until I realize how it unfurls. I roll it down the rock-hard shaft.

Adam lifts my hips and has me sit on top. He uses his cock to tease me, rubbing it front and back. My cunt is dripping and his penis is sliding effortlessly between my vulva. Finally, he pulls me down and I gasp. Holy fuck. The entire length of his substantial cock is now buried deep inside. My vagina quivers and I cum. How is this even possible?

Adam is relentless now. He is moving me back and forth. I suspect I will be bruised from where he is holding my hips. He presses me downward at an angle so my clit is rubbing on his pubic bone, the cunt juice making it a perfect slippery platform. I cum again and then again, waves and waves building. He throws me down and rolls on top. I am overwhelmed by his size and strength. I feel taken, slave to her master. He pounds into me. I feel I might split in two. He hikes my legs up high and dives deeper and deeper. I sense he may be close to climaxing. I close my eyes and give into the sensation. I cum, loudly, furiously like an animal. He brings his mouth to my ear and says, "Such a good pet you are. I am very pleased." He presses down, his arms snaking over my shoulders for greater leverage. Adam gives into the moment, his rhythm persistent. I again close my eyes and focus on the sensation, his breath, his muscular body, his substantial cock, and for the umpteenth time, I cum. I hear his breath quicken and I feel his cock pulsing as he explodes in orgasm. It's the stuff of movies, only it's real life.

Adam, rolls to one side. He pulls me over his chest and draws his arm over me. With his left hand, he tips my head so my eyes meet his. "Very good, my pet. You have pleased me." He closes his eyes and strokes my hair. We drift off together.

I waken when Adam turns me over on my side. His erection is pressed against my back and buttocks. He slides into my vagina, my labia swollen from our initial romp. He slowly and methodically moves in and out, his left hand draped over my hip and focused on my crotch. My clit swells into a perfect sphere. It's the most agonizing sex. I am close to cumming but the rhythm is too slow to bring me to climax. I sense he is teasing me.

Suddenly, he pulls out and stands me up against a wall facing away from him. He kicks my legs out so I widen my stance. He pulls my hips toward him and he dives in from behind. He is ruthless now. Fucking me hard, like I am a blow-up doll. He pulls on my breasts, bites my back and neck, slaps my thighs, and pounds into me. Finally, both his hands zero in on my clit. The left hand spreads my labia. The right hand works in circles and with downward strokes. It's a furious attack, and they bring me to orgasm and hold me there. In a hoarse voice, I say, "I am cumming, I am cumming, please don't stop, I am still cumming." And he doesn't stop. It's only when my whole body shudders and my legs give out that he relents.

He picks me up and carries me to the edge of the bed, laying me back with my buttocks hanging off in space. He places one of my feet on each of his shoulders and dives in again. I am so wet, there are silly squishing sounds with each thrust. This excites him no end. He tells me over and over, "I want to make you wet." He pushes me back further on the bed, pressing down on my shins, legs folded. He pushes them sideways, exposing my clit completely. Over and over, in and out, slow and then fast, Adam fucks me like an Olympic Gold Medalist. Waves of orgasms wash over me and my cunt juice forms a puddle. The wetter I get, the more determined he is to make me cum again.

He swoops down to pick me up, his arms laced under mine, hands turned over to control my shoulders. He lifts me up and then lets gravity pull me down. He is so deep inside, I feel I might burst. He now cups my ass, my arms around his neck. He fucks me hard. I sense he may be close, so I tightened my cunt. Already swollen from so much fucking, this last bit is too much for him to resist. He explodes in waves. I feel his body shudder and his cock shake. He lays me on my back and he rolls over to lay beside me. Pleasure and pain, oh my God, who knew?

Aftercare this time was a double shower. I washed his body and he washed mine. We curled up together and slept in each other's arms. I had never felt so close to anyone, and truthfully, I barely knew Adam. He was definitely some years younger, but in no way boyish. I wondered how much he was paid or even if he was paid. Such a strange arrangement, and yet I felt so close and connected.

The ride home left me in a dream-state. I closed off the windows between my driver and myself completely. I wanted to be alone with my thoughts. I wondered if I will ever have this kind of intimacy in the course of a relationship? I mean, I have no time for dating, and the agreement with S was no outside relationship or sex with anyone else during my "journey." I definitely felt more alive than I have perhaps ever felt. But at the same time, I felt no more clarity than I did on day one. Hmmm.

S said she wouldn't be able to see me this week but that she had something very special planned for Saturday. The hint of things to come was forefront in my mind but I managed to solve the issue with the IPO and it went through. I am good at making money. Damn straight.

Finally, Saturday arrives, and again I head out the door filled with excitement. I envisioned more of the same luscious love making. The usual assistant takes me to the dressing room. There seems to be more of a buzz in the House of S with doors opening and closing. I even see a few other "clients" in the halls.

The outfit laid out for me is the Barbarella one. (If you haven't seen the Jane Fonda classic, you must. So campy.) In my mind, this is cave girl attire. It wraps around, exposing one breast, one buttock, and most of my crotch, and no thong this time. The assistant also fastens a collar, a leather one that seems all business. She wraps me in the kimono and then has me sit down so she can pull my hair up into a ponytail. She ties it with a long piece of leather, wrapping the leather around and around so the ponytail stands tall and high like a horse's tail that's been broken and set.

There's a knock on the door, and a voice says, "It's time." The assistant attaches a leash to my collar and begins to walk me down the hall and then into the elevator two floors down into the basement. While it's dimly lit, I can see people have already gathered. Women and men are in the center, tethered to posts by their leashes. An assistant is securing hands behind their backs and spreader bars to their ankles. Shit. What the fuck?

My assistant's last official act is to remove my kimono. She hands me off to a man who leads me to a post. I stand exposed. Once secured, he cuffs my hands behind me and then smacks my legs so I stand wide. Clip, clip, he attaches the spreader bar.

I look up, hoping to see Adam. Instead, I see a crowd of people, but only just barely. All the lights in the room are trained on those of us tethered and on display. People are taking seats. I look around. There must be ten of us at least.

To say I feel awkward is an understatement. I was used to being exposed with Adam. I had no idea that I, Catherine Standish Bolton, would ever be on display in front of a room full of people. God, I hoped and prayed no one would recognize me. Surely, S would have taken care somehow…

An announcer steps up to the center to my left, microphone in hand. "Ladies and gentlemen, inspections will start momentarily. May I remind you that a substantial deposit secures your right to one hour with a slave. If you are satisfied, you may complete your purchase.

Fuck, this is an auction, and I am an item. I just closed a $300,000,000 IPO and here I am, for sale. For fuck's sake.

S and Adam are nowhere to be seen. The crowd of "buyers" begin milling about. A fifty-something man with manicured hands approaches. I lower my head, not from any desire to be demure but in hopes he does not recognize me. He runs his hands along my body. When I pull away, he hits my cheek with the back of his hand. I look up in shock and horror, and he strikes me again. Fuck. Shit got real.

Others come by to inspect. A woman runs her hand, thumb-side up, between my legs. She smells her hand and smiles. She cups my butt in her hands and squeezes before she moves on to inspect others.

I have never felt so belittled and yet so excited in all my life. I am on display as something that can be bought -- naked, exposed -- and I find this moment thrilling. Am I out of my mind?

The announcer takes the mic, "Ladies and gentlemen, you have fifteen minutes to place bids. Please complete your inspections. Remember: Should your winning bid be within $100 of the next lowest bid, your slave is subject to live auction to the highest bidder."

I am helpless. Shackled, tied to a post, and basically naked, the high-powered mistress of her universe is about to be sold.

The auctioneer calls out a number, slave #1, and the lights focus on someone to the far left. A winner is announced. The winner rises and the slave is led off to meet her fate. This process continues through slave #8, directly to my left. The lights now focus on me. I feel the warmth of four spotlights on my bare skin. I want to cry out, to scream. I want to say, "I am Catherine Standish Bolton, fucking mistress of her universe, you morons." For my sake, I manage to stay quiet. The auctioneer's assistant steps up and uses a crop to lift my chin. I see only the bright white light, but I know just beyond what I can see are dozens of people, one of whom will soon own me.

Well, wouldn't you know it? Two bids within $100. I am the first to be live auctioned. I am about to find out what I am worth. The bidding starts at $2,500, a miniscule fraction of my net worth. The action heats up and soon the price is over $5,000. Two voices seem to be in hot contention - one female and one male.

The pace is slowing down at $7,000, but neither party is willing to cede the win. The auctioneer pauses and makes this announcement, "Ladies and gentlemen, clearly this slave is equally valued by our two bidders. I am offering the opportunity to stop bidding and grant both of you equal time access to this slave for today. Do you agree?"

What? Shared by two? Apparently, the two parties agree, because the male auction assistant comes over to remove my restraints and to lead me out to the right. I am handed off to another assistant and lead unceremoniously down the hall and ushered into a room. There, waiting for me is the woman who had done the rather close inspection. The assistant hands my leash to her and leaves.

The woman drops my leash and steps over to lock the door. She pulls up her dress and slips off her lacy underwear. She positions herself on the bed, legs apart, and says, "Get to it."

Wow. I am a bit slow to respond. I have never been intimate with a woman and yet I am about to go down on one. She senses my hesitancy and says, "Do I need to discipline you first?" I shake my head no and move over to the bed.

To buy time, I start by kissing her inner thighs and making small, rather gentle bites. I place my forearms under her thighs and slide my hands up toward her hips. I decide to move closer to her clit but to continue teasing her, licking, kissing, and nibbling in ever smaller circles. I then go all-in, I press my tongue on the space just behind her hymen and press in and pull up in one long lick. She moans. Good. I do this two more times, pressing slightly harder each time. On the third pass, I stop at her clit, which has now swelled to a lovely, perky sphere. I suck it in between my teeth and press my tongue firmly. I move my mouth in circles pulling the clit along with me. She is moaning non-stop at this point.

I change positions to lay alongside her and slide my right hand into her crotch, smacking it hard against her clit. She exhales sharply. I slide my middle finger into her cunt and rub it back and forth against the front wall. I alternate this with the whole hand hitting her clit and cunt. She is squirming and pulling my hair.

I see a bowl of warm coconut oil on the side table and decide to bump it up a notch still. I pull out my finger and thrust it into the bowl and then, dripping in oil, I move back to her ass. I use the knuckle of my index finger to press in gently and move in small circles. I look up at her face, and she is clearly transported to another space. Her eyes are rolled back and her mouth is open. I begin to slide my middle finger into her ass slowly. I see her cunt opening and dripping pearl-colored juice. I rub the front wall of her rectum and take my mouth to her clit. I move down with my tongue, lapping up the free-flowing juice. She loses it at this point, and cunt juice squirts into my face and puddles beneath her.

I am not sure what to do next. The woman still has her eyes closed, so I gently retract my finger and raise my head. I decide I should give my hands a good scrub. When I turn back, her eyes are open and coming into focus. "I am sorry for your sake, but I still have some energy. Come here." I am confused by the combination of these two sentences, but I do what I am told.

She takes my leash and ties it to the bedpost so that I am bent over if I am standing. I go to sit down and she says, "Tisk, tisk. No, my girl. Stand up. Or should I say, bend over."

She adjusts my positioning so she is squarely facing my ass. Out of nowhere, comes a hard whack on my right cheek. She strikes my left buttock with the same paddle. (Where did this paddle come from?) I don't make a sound: I am in shock. Soon, however, the relentless paddling becomes so painful, I am crying out with each hit. My cries only seem to encourage her. My flesh is on fire, and unlike Adam's strikes, she is not pulling back at all.

I am not sure how many hits I have taken, but my right knee begins to buckle, and I go down. This is met with a slap to my face and I force myself up. Finally, after several rounds like this, she sits down in an adjacent chair. I am now on my knees, head hung down, panting like an animal. She is apparently pleased with her work.

There's a knock at the door, and the woman looks at her watch. "My, how time flies." She adjusts her clothing and abruptly leaves. I am still tethered to the bed, my ass covered in welts, and tracks of tears down my face.

My usual assistant comes in and attempts to get me onto the bed. She leaves to get someone to help her. They manage to get me laying down on my stomach with ice packs on my backside. My assistant gently brushes my hair and gathers it back up into a ponytail. She washes my face with a cool cloth. The other assistant replaces the ice packs. At this point, my assistant whispers into my ear, "The man who is coming is a regular. As soon as you can, get his cock in your mouth. He won't want to hit you if you disarm him like this." With that, the two leave. I decide I should hide my damaged ass for fear the sight of it will ignite some animal fire in this new master.

I sit on the edge of the bed, pushing my chest out. My hope is to look fetching and sexy enough to get this new master straight into sex. The door opens and a short, balding, middle-aged man with a paunch steps in. Damn. He is the least attractive partner I can imagine. It's going to have to take every ruse I have to move him in the right direction. Impulsively, I stand up rather quickly and walk over and kneel at his feet. I reach out my hands and begin to stroke his legs. As my hands move to his inner thigh, I raise my face. He is looking at me quizzically. I raise up enough to have my face level with his crotch. I press into it and breathe out warm, moist air. My hands are up at his belt, slipping off the clasp. I unbutton his pants and slowly unzip. His pants drop to around his ankles. I pull down his boxers and there is the smallest, least attractive penis I have ever confronted. Fuck.

I close my eyes and begin to pull and tug on this sad organ with my mouth. I slip my hands around to his buttocks where I run my fingers back and forth. Slowly, slowly his cock comes alive. I stand up and lead him to the bed, helping him step out of his clothes. I walk backwards, facing him, keeping my red smarting ass out of view.

I lay him down and look him over like the most prized possession I have ever known. I return to his cock and between my hands and mouth it's now fully erect, all of four, maybe five inches. Damn. This poor man. What a lot in life.

I ask him, "Master, what do you desire? How can I serve you?" From his eyes, I can see this excites him. He fumbles in his coat pocket and pulls out a condom. I tear the packet with my teeth and unroll it onto his penis while stroking his balls. I am terrified he will lose his erection.

"Master, how do you want it?" His eyes flash.

"I will fuck you in your ass."

I am terrified he will turn me over and see/feel my red butt. I honestly don't think I can take any more. I decide I will manage this feat from on top. "Master, may I please sit on your cock? It would please me so, if you will allow this." He nods eagerly. I say a silent thank you to my assistant who literally may have saved my ass today. Once again, I dip my hand into the warm coconut oil. I slather it all over his cock, speaking to it as though it has a life of its own. *So beautiful. What a wonder you are. Can I ever manage to take you inside? You are so big.*

I straddle master #2 and manage to slip his dick inside my ass. It's an easy fit and not unpleasant, like one or two fingers sliding in and out. I ooh and aaah at appropriate moments, especially when the sensation is genuinely pleasant. I close my eyes and think of Adam. This helps. I am no longer fucking a dumpy man whom I am NOT attracted to. Instead, I am overpowered and commanded to perform by the most amazing partner I have ever known. It doesn't take long before master #2 cums. Now what?

I swing into action. I unbutton his shirt and rub his chest in the most erotic way, dipping down to suck his nipples. I move to sit behind his head, massaging his scalp and face. I allow my breasts to loom close to his face. I keep up this whole charade for what seems like hours. I am not sure how long he has claim to me but I am certain he will not be spanking me.

I get this wild idea, like totally out of left field. I look around. That paddle must be here somewhere. I spy it on an adjacent table. I stand up and fetch it. When I return, my voice changes, "Turn over." My words are the words of Catherine Standish Bolton, bad-ass financier. "Turn over like a good boy." To my surprise, he complies. I tell him, "You've been a naughty boy, haven't you? You've been thinking naughty thoughts. You've been doing naughty things. You've been a very bad boy." And then, I lay into him, spanking each cheek in turn, over and over. His skin turns pink and then red. I tell him he needs to be punished for being such a bad boy. And I spank him some more.

He doesn't cry out. In fact, he seems relieved. I pause to take stock of the situation. Embolden, I roll him over, "Bad boys need to make amends, don't they? And YOU have been very bad indeed." I sit down and lean back, legs spread. "You will lick me. You will lick me until I am satisfied. Do you understand?" Dumpy guy nods vigorously. I close my eyes and let him work himself into a frenzy, all the while visualizing Adam attacking me like a lion pouncing on a gazelle. I manage to cum, and when the dumpy guy looks up, chin covered in my goo, I give him a stern look. He interprets this correctly and gets back to work.

Finally, there is a knock at the door. Thank God, this day is coming to an end. Master #2 smiles sheepishly at me as he leaves. I feel I have found my new self. Bad-ass bitch.

When I reach home, there, as always, is a note from S.

Catherine,

Your head must be swimming in thoughts. Let these swim through. And as your feelings and judgments surface, let these go as well.

Tonight, celebrate this new dynamic that emerged with champagne. I have tucked a bit of caviar into the bag as the perfect accompaniment.

S

I tell my house manager to get champagne from the wine cooler, a bottle of Veuve Clicquot, along with my favorite Arte Nouveau champagne flute. I hand her the bag from S and tell her to have the chef lay out a nice spread before he turns in for the night.

Thirty minutes later, I am lounging in my favorite armchair, feet up on an ottoman, appreciating how soft the seat is considering the state of my backside. It will be an arnica night, but first champagne and caviar call.

On Monday, I find myself unusually focused at work. There is a large deal on the table and I am determined to make it happen. That's what I do. I make things happen. My assistant interrupts to confirm appointments for the week. When she gets to Wednesday's schedule, I realize I haven't thought of the House of S all morning.

Wednesday evening, as I pull up to the brownstone, I step out of the car feeling, well, different. Hmmm.

S greets me warmly and suggests we sample some vintage red wine with a rich English cheddar. Does she spoil all her clients this way? Seated in the two facing chairs, sipping the rich red, I feel relaxed, at ease. I cannot remember when I felt this way.

"So what are your thoughts, Catherine? What are you learning?"

I pause, take in a breath, look out through the gauzy blinds to the street below. "S, where is Adam?"

"He is here, Catherine."

"Can I see him?"

"Why?"

"I would just like to see him."

"One should always explore one's motivations. These reveal so much. And, it may be possible for you to see him. I can have someone check his schedule while we talk."

Instead of answers, I find I have only questions. "Why the auction, S? Did you engineer it so I would be bought by not one, but two people?"

"Engineer it? No. I let clients act out their dreams and passions as they unfold. How did it feel to be exposed, sized up, and purchased?"

"I thought I would hate it. It runs counter to everything I thought I believed in. And yet, part of me enjoyed being fought over, though I have to say, had I known the dumpy guy was one of the highest bidders, I would have felt less pride!"

"Ah yes, Mr. Smith, a regular here. What did you learn from your encounter with him?"

"I think I came back to the self I know best, the part that takes command and runs the show. That felt comfortable. I struggled horribly with his appearance, but I found strategies to overcome that. That's what I do. I find ways of overcoming."

"Yes, Catherine, you do. No doubt of that. And the female client? How was that for you?"

"So that experience was interesting on two counts. First, it was like making love to myself. I did to her what I would like done to me. I enjoyed watching the impact it had on her. Second, I felt truly helpless when she was spanking me so brutally. She had none of Adam's finesse."

"I take it you have never been with a woman before. How was it to be with the same sex?"

"In this situation, it simply felt like a task. But I can imagine that with the right woman, it would be wonderful."

There was a knock at the door. S told whomever it was to enter. To my delight, Adam stepped in.

S smiled and said, "Well, Adam. I believe Catherine wants to speak to you. My assistant will show her out. I have to check on something, so you will be able to speak privately for maybe 15 minutes. Catherine, is that enough time?"

I smile back and say, "Yes, of course." S closes the door behind her. I bolt to Adam, expecting him to greet me with open arms. Instead, he threads his left hand into my hair near the roots, controlling my head.

"Missed me, did you? Then you can show your devotion." With that, he presses downward till I am kneeling before his crotch, his penis clearly swelling beneath his leather briefs.

Not exactly what I expected but I will take it. I unfasten the fly and slide his briefs down enough to fully expose his balls and fully erect cock. I haven't ever seen his cock with this much light before. It is a thing of beauty, perfectly proportioned and on the large side. The head is a luscious pink and the shaft slightly tanner. His pubic hair is neatly trimmed and the base of his penis and his balls are hairless. I go to work.

Adam threads his right hand into my hair so he fully controls my head. He tells me to grab his ass with both hands and he proceeds to fuck my mouth rather ruthlessly. I adjust the tilt of my head slightly to lessen the desire to gag with each thrust. Adam treats me like a blow-up doll, solely focused on his own pleasure. I decide to accept the situation and begin experimenting with my tongue, teeth, and lips. At one point, my teeth graze his skin. He yanks my head back with his left hand and slaps me hard with his right. Grabbing my hair again, he continues to fuck my mouth hard and deep. I gag a bit and furiously press my neck back and upwards to lengthen my mouth. Unlike his usual prolonged love-making, Adam allows himself to climax quickly. He pulls out and sprays cum all over my face. "Eat it," he says. "I want you to eat it all." Dutifully, I use my fingers to sweep the slippery goo into my mouth. He fastens his briefs and smiles. "Come, sit at my feet."

Adam moves over to one of the chairs, pointing to a spot next to him on the floor. Wow, this really isn't what I imagined at all. Still, I know the penalty for non-compliance. I quickly move and sit. He again grabs my hair with his left hand and tilts my head upwards. "Such a good girl. You pleased me today." As I start to smile, I am taken aback by another hard slap to my right cheek. "You need to always please me, Catherine."

Closing his eyes, he then tilts his head back and begins to stroke my hair. In a few minutes, he sits up, kisses the top of my head, and then pulls me into his lap. He caresses my breasts through my shirt and kisses me passionately. He briefly slides his hand under my skirt, heading straight for my pussy. When he finds it wet, he smiles, and says, "Yes, that's my good girl. If you continue to be a good girl, I will fuck you soon, but only if you are good. You will be good, Catherine, won't you?" I nod vigorously. I am desperate in the moment for him to fuck me.

Adam, lifts me up and sets me on my feet. He holds my head to his chest with one hand while the other cups my ass. He presses into me. And then, like that, he leaves.

I left the House of S in a complete tizzy. Shit. Fuck. Damn. Maybe seeing Adam wasn't such a good idea. Why had I wanted to see him anyway? S had asked and I had dodged the question. Why was that? What had I expected?

I arrive home and head straight to the bar to make a drink. I am beyond tempted to call one or more of my casual lovers. My agreement with the House of S was no outside sex. I am feeling the desperate need for affirmation of some kind. As though the universe were perfect, the bell rings and my assistant comes in to say I have a visitor. Really? She hands me a calling card with the elegant S scribed across the front. Hmmm. I tell her to show the visitor in.

If things couldn't get any more surprising, she shows in a gorgeous, petite, and somewhat demure thirty-something female. I thank her and tell her I will ring if we need anything. Beyond curious, I extend my hand to my surprise guest, who, instead of reaching back, lowers her hand and eyes with a slight bow. "I am Sheila. I am yours to do with as you wish, ma'am."

Wow. I take two more long gulps of my drink and then muster, "Very well, Sheila. You're a good girl, aren't you?" I can see her smile but she is trained well and doesn't raise her head. I set my glass down and step over, grabbing her hair close to her scalp I tilt her head up. "Look at me." She does, green eyes shining, looking to read my reactions.

"Very well, Sheila. Come this way. In full-sub fashion, she walks two paces behind. I take her to my bedroom suite. "Take off your clothes." She starts by slipping off her pencil skirt, revealing a grey leather and lace thong. She unbuttons each button of her sleeveless shirt in a lyrical fashion. She has had practice and training in how to be alluring. I find myself getting wet between my legs as her slender fingers move from button to button, sliding down the placket of the shirt. She is wearing a halter-bra, ideal for controlling her upper body. She stands before me - high heels, thong, halter bra, and a polished-aluminum collar.

I feel desire well up. She is mine for the plucking and I will have her. "Turn around slowly." She complies, and her ass, round and muscular comes into full view. Yum. I lock my door. I do this for effect only. It's not necessary. No one will dare enter.

"Undress me." Sheila confidently moves to this task, removing my shirt while expertly brushing her hands in delightful ways against bare skin. Back of the hand against my shoulder. Forearm sweeping across my stomach. I am dripping at this point.

She faces me inches away and unzips my skirt. Instead of removing it, she moves her hand down to my crotch, smiling as her fingers slide into a pool of wetness that is my vagina. She slips a wet finger to my swollen clit and begins massaging it. Damn, she is good.

She pauses to slide down my skirt. She bends down to slip off my low-heeled pumps, kissing the tops of my feet. I grab the back of her harness and haul her up roughly. I shove her in front of me toward the bed, yanking her to a stop. I spin her around and grab her breasts and then reach around to her amazing ass and pull her toward me, kissing her roughly. I suck on her lips, bite, engulf. I treat her like a possession. I push her back and then down and pull her into my crotch. This pet knows just what to do. It's like she studied my playbook from last weekend. I am awash in cunt juice and moans.

I roll over and stuff two pillows under my hips, thrusting my ass into the air. She dives in licking my butt while driving her fingers into my cunt. I cum repeatedly. She continues her task without stopping until I just can't stand it anymore.

"Did you bring any toys with you?" She nods. "Get them." She goes to her bag and pulls out a matching leather strap-on and several attachments. My eyes grow large when I see a massive dildo of nearly impossible size. "Put it on me with this." I hand her the massive tool. She discreetly pulls out a jar, opens it, and puts it on the nightstand. I smell the familiar odor of coconut oil.

Soon I am strapped in with a massive dildo hanging in front. I grab her harness, bend her over, and push her face into a pile of pillows. I kick her legs apart. I slather coconut oil on the dildo and her pink asshole that looks rather like pursed lips. I circle the tip of the dildo on her asshole, then slap her butt with my hand. I press in gently and she opens up. I feel the dildo sliding in. I stay at the edge, just moving the head in and out very slowly. When she begins to moan, I push deeper and deeper. Then I pull out nearly the full length and again slide all the way in. This is making her crazy. My own cunt is swollen and soaking wet, so much so the juice begins to run down my leg. I reach around to put both hands on her crotch. One works her clit and the other edges around her cunt. I fuck her for ten minutes like this as she cums repeatly.

I leave her in a heap on the bed and I go wash the dildo thoroughly. I have plans.

I come back. She opens her eyes and smiles. I slip her into the strap-on and adjust it to her smaller frame. I spread my feet and bend over the edge of the bed. She dives in with her face and licks my ass with a firm, persistent tongue. I melt. She coats the dildo with coconut oil and presses it against my ass. I immediately open up and she slowly slides it all the way in. She works my clit in furious circles as she moves in and out, slowly at first. Soon, she is pounding me like a teenager as I cum for several minutes that feel like years. It is glorious and overwhelming. My ass aches from the sheer size of the dildo, so I push her out and flop on the bed. "Take off the strap-on and lay beside me." She does. We cuddle and kiss like school girls at a same-sex boarding school. I consider the day's events. There are no words.

I wake up hours later and she is still next to me. I think of her like a pet, a kitten, warm, cuddly, in need of direction. I snap to and ask myself this question: "What the fuck, Catherine? I mean, really, what the fuck are you doing?" I wake up the kitten gently and ask her if she needs a ride home. She shakes her head no, telling me a car has been waiting for her. She asks if she is dismissed. Yes, kitten, you need to go so I can think. She gets dressed and I see her out.

I head to the kitchen and make myself a cup of tea. Maybe the answers will magically appear in the swirling leaves. Of course, no answers appear, only questions, so many questions.

What on earth am I doing? That seems to be a big one.

How is this helping me? Oh, and that one, too.

Then there's: *Who do I think I am fooling?*

Somehow, I hear my mother's voice in all this, the voice of someone who cares but who also judges rather harshly. She (my mother) died some years back. I say she died from lack of inspiration, but I think the medical diagnosis was a stroke, thus my annual check-ups, scans, and reassurances that are never all that reassuring.

My mother was the dominant voice in my family. My father, while the designated bread-winner, seemed to lack balls while my mother had more than enough to pronounce judgment on anyone and anything. Damn, would I ever be able to rid myself of her voice in my head?

I decide I am going to go for a walk. Never mind that it's in the wee hours of the morning. I need to think. I throw on sneakers and my favorite yoga pants and camisole and head out. The air is heavy tonight, feels like a storm might be moving in. It's that time when the pressure gradients meet and the air hangs for a while before the incoming front wins the battle and the wind starts up. The heavy air feels like a metaphor: I am still very much stuck. The new wind hasn't moved out the old energy. I resolve to reconnect with Brad. I need someone to help me process the events of the last few weeks.

On Sunday, I email my assistant to make an appointment with Brad as soon as possible. I also message S directly, saying I need a week to think. Relieved for the moment, I spend the day in my favorite comfort corner and chair, catching up on financial news.

My assistant worked her usual magic and I have an appointment with Brad for Monday at 6 pm. I manage to take charge of my Monday in the usual "Catherine-fashion", directing staff to handle countless matters. Everything at work is, thankfully, sorted and moving ahead. Bolton Financial remains a force to be reckoned with. I remind myself that I am, too.

My driver gets me to Brad's office in no time. I arrive a few minutes early, Just enough time for me to think of where I want to start, but...Brad (apparently) didn't have an appointment before mine, so he steps out to greet me warmly. "Catherine, I am surprised to see you, but, of course, also delighted. Please, come in."

I settle into the client's chair, somewhat smaller than Brad's chair and positioned in such a way to set up a power differential. Here, the client is diminutive. I wonder if I even would have noticed this before.

"So, Catherine, what do you want to talk about, or should I say, talk through?"

I take a deep breath and wonder where to even start. "I have lived several lifetimes in the past month."

"Is that good or bad, Catherine?"

"I don't know that the experiences themselves are good or bad - I mean, they just 'are'".

"Ah, I appreciate the lack of judgment here. Do you think you would have felt this way earlier on? If you had a friend who had had those same experiences, would you have judged them?"

"Absolutely. No doubt at all. I would have attempted to get my friend help. Like professional help. I would have thought them crazy for trying any of this."

"But you're not crazy, are you, Catherine?"

"No, no, I don't think so, but I am questioning this process. It's not like in the moment I am questioning anything. Each experience has been, well, FULLY engaging. I do realize that that is an important part of living -- experiencing fully each moment -- and one I was lacking in my world. I mean, so much of what I do is around betting on a future. I spend my work days looking at trends and forecasts. So, yes, being pulled into every moment is a new experience for me. And the range of feelings has been extraordinary. I rarely feel overwhelmed in "my world" and I regularly feel completely off-balance in the House of S."

"Catherine, feeling off balance means at some point you will find your footing again. And when you do, where do you think that will leave you?"

"I cannot even begin to answer that question. I am at once ecstatic, horrified, delighted, and disgusted. I mean, Brad, I was auctioned as a slave. Someone paid money for my time. Not money I ever saw. Compared to my net worth, it was a pittance. And yet, I went along. I assumed the role. That is some crazy shit."

I raised my hand to stop Brad from speaking and continued, "I cannot reconcile this. I consider myself a liberated woman. Look at my life. Look at what I've accomplished. How can I reconcile that against allowing myself to become a slave, to be demeaned, and then to turn around and demean others? I mean, I am fundamentally questioning my inherent goodness." I sat back, crossed my legs, and folded my hands in my lap. I had finally given voice to my angst.

"Hmmm. Catherine, what is it to be liberated? What does that mean? Is it a set of behaviors and accomplishments or is it, perhaps, an openness, a stance that says all experience has value in shaping a person? I mean, look up the definition of the word, liberated. You'll see phrases like 'free from limits, boundaries.' Haven't you gone past boundaries you may not have even known you had?" He set his eyes on me intensely.

"Okay, so maybe the idea of liberation I held was a bit limited, but I am still struggling with the concept of slavery."

"Catherine, at any point did you lose sight of your choice in that scene? At any point, did you think you had given up control over your life completely?"

"Of course not. I mean, I've never tried to bolt. I haven't even used my safe word."

"Okay, so what is the difference between being a slave in a scene and being a slave in life? I would even go so far as to say you ARE a slave in life. You, Catherine Standish Bolton, are a slave to the company you built." It was his turn to sit back and cross his arms.

Okay, so I didn't see that coming. Yes, I had given everything to Bolton Financial. I had stayed single. Childless. I built a fortress that was both awesome in its magnitude and power and desperate in its isolation and loneliness. I had taken pride in what I had built. I never considered weighing that against what I had given up in the process.

"I don't know where to go from here. Honestly, I am lost."

"Catherine, you are not lost. In fact, I think you are on the way to being found. You feel lost because the journey isn't complete. To become something new means you have to shed old things that no longer serve you. You just don't know what those are just yet."

I feel a tear falling down my cheek. And then another. The tears fall like a persistent gentle rain, the kind of rain one hopes for as a gardener. The kind of rain that brings needed moisture but doesn't wash away shallow sprouting seeds. I hope the seeds sprouting in me will bear fruit soon. I do not like this murky place in between.

I ring S on the way back home and leave a message. I've changed my mind. I don't need to take a break. I end the call and wonder if that's really true. Am I ready for what's next?

S is something of a mind-reader. She has this uncanny ability to read me. It's unnerving and comforting at the same time. When I reach home, I see a card embossed with the iconic S on the tray of drinks (tea, water, white wine) that are always ready to greet me. I love that my house manager sees no point in wasting time finding out what I want. She simply has my favorite options ready...all of them.

I choose the chablis and take one delicious sip and then open the envelope. In her unmistakable handwriting is a rather long note:

Catherine,

You may be feeling unnerved, even shaken at this point. While it's hard to imagine, that's a good sign. It means you are getting ready to make a shift. Inner movement has detectable signs on the outside. Whenever someone wants to pause or stop, they are on a cusp of a breakthrough. Having said that, some breakthroughs are quite subtle. I am not promising fireworks or the enlightenment of the Buddha. Still, while you may not see it, I am certain you are getting ready, ready for what's next.

I also imagine you are a bit shocked how easy it's been for you to slide into different roles. You may not recognize that you have done this your whole life. I have no doubt that much of the success of Bolton Financial lies in your ability to shift and change as circumstances demand.

I do know you are most comfortable being in charge. Remember, you cannot fully know who you are without experiencing the flip side - submission - and not just casually, but in a deep and illuminating way. If you give yourself to this fully, you may find a bliss you didn't know was possible.

So, Catherine, just know, I am here for you. Every decision I make is in response to your needs. The fact that you are questioning yourself deeply right now simply means I have hit the mark.

S

God, I feel like such a child when I read S's notes. She is so calm, so measured. I, on the other hand, am torn up and conflicted to the core. I long for the peace she radiates.

I wake to a text from S, suggesting no meeting this week. I am just to show up on Saturday at 10. Okay then. Here we go, or should I say, here I go.

The week flies by. I am (blessedly) consumed by many details related to some short sales and one regulatory inquiry. I am happy to have these distractions. It keeps me from wondering what awaits me on Saturday.

And yes, Saturday comes. I wake up, mouth dry, more questions than answers. I change up my outfit, skinny jeans and a white buttondown blouse over a sports bra. I change my hair, brushing it up and back. I so want to be the bad bitch today, the one who can take it all and more.

The door to the House of S swings open and my sweet escort, ever ready to get me sorted, greets me. She takes note of my new look and says, "Wow, Catherine, you look, well... confident." Not exactly 'bad bitch' but I'll take confident.

She takes me to a changing room and shows me a two-part harness in red leather. It clearly allows for whomever to manage me physically. To my surprise, I feel ever more the bad bitch as I strap in. I look in the full-length mirror, breasts outlined by red straps, ass framed by leg and waist straps. The upper harness has one length of leather up my spine that connects to a collar. Yes, I make a magnificent pet.

My escort takes out my pony tail. My hair is to fall free today, better for grabbing and pulling, I suspect. She clicks in a matching red leash. I am tempted to hold it between my teeth the way a poodle who wants to go for a walk might.

There's a knock and my heart skips a beat as Adam opens the door with a look of admiration. The assistant quickly wraps me in my kimono, and hands my leash to Adam, who carries it loosely over his right shoulder. The leash is now more of a symbol than any real means of control. I have willingly given into his spell. Fuck, Catherine. The web has you and the eyes of the spider seem glorious and mesmerizing.

Adam ushers us into a splendid space. It's dominated by a king bed with the most luscious purple satin duvet and a ridiculous number of pillows. He peels off the robe and lets it drop to the ground. "Catherine, today, you will wholly be mine." Oh. My. God. I am instantly wet between the legs and aching for him. "Lay down." I oblige willingly.

Adam, surveys the landscape, and in short order removes what little clothing he is wearing. He has the most magnificent erection. The profile of his body against the dim, diffused light is near perfection. He straddles my upper body, sitting on my chest. I am now face-to-face with his cock. He presents it like an offering. I open my mouth, hungry to bring him pleasure. My clit swells. He fucks my mouth with such mastery that right as I think I might gag, he has pulled back. I realize I am able to take more and more of him in without issue. He is training me and I am happy to be the good student.

He then slides off and lays beside me, his mouth goes to my right breast. He sucks on the nipple hard. It's at the edge of pleasure becoming pain. He is unrelenting, moving to the left breast and back to the right, over and over, until my nipples are ridiculously erect and hard. His right hand smacks against my clit and pubic bone. An audible moan leaves my lips. Holy fuck.

He pulls his head back and gives me a sidelong glance, "My, my, my pet, you are ready, aren't you?" I blush. I am so fucking wet even his finger is making swishing sounds. He pulls his finger out of my cunt and moves to my ass. "I will fuck all your holes today." Rather than a threat, I take comfort in that promise. I will be taken and it will be glorious.

He uses the harness to reposition me on all fours. He pauses to slip on a condom and hands me the bowl of warmed coconut oil. I know what this means. I dip in three fingers and coat his now massive erection with the yummy oil. I turn back and slide my hand to my clit. He presses against my ass, and I open up to him easily, completely, effortlessly. As he moves in and out, my hand makes persistent circles over my clit, pressing against the public bone. I begin to cum. Instead of allowing it to rise and subside quickly, I adjust my pace to build to a plateau where I moan, "I am cumming, I am cumming. Please don't stop." This goes on for what feels like minutes. Juice from my vagina drips down my legs. I am in bliss. Rapture. The world could end and I wouldn't care. I have never experienced anything like this before.

Adam gently pulls out and lays me on my back. He smiles, "One moment, my pet," and he steps to the vanity to remove the condom and wash up. He returns and hands me another one. I smile and confidently unfurl it over his cock. I pause to give it a suck or five, sliding my mouth and hand down the full length. I feel it swell even more.

Adam, grabs my chest harness and presses me into the bed. "Legs up, my horny slave. Show me how much you want me." Oh, lord. Catherine Standish Bolton, raises her legs, knees bent, and spreads open her labia. My cunt is a mouth waiting to consume him. He teases me, circling the head of penis outside my vagina, then moving it up and down from clit to hymen. My eyes roll back into my head. "Fuck me. Fuck me, please. Fuck me, please, master."

Those were the words he was apparently waiting for. He slides in and presses his body against mine, occasionally using my legs to adjust position or height. I am completely lost in all this. The world dissolves and it is just Adam and me. I would do anything for him at this point. I am beyond willing.

He lays down and slides his hands under, up, and over my shoulders and starts fucking me hard. I draw my legs up even higher, exposing my clit to his relentless pounding. I reach climax after climax and I feel he is close. This makes me crazy. I want him to melt into me. As he cums, he presses his mouth to my ear and says, "Catherine... you...are...mine." I explode along with him and I milk the last of his cum and my orgasm by closing my legs tightly around him and moving his body against my pubic bone.

Never in my life...that's the phrase running through my mind on a loop...never in my life. I have never felt so close to someone. Yet, I hardly know Adam. I have never been so willing to let someone else lead. Yet, here I am, willingly his slave. I have never let myself experience or even seek such pleasure. Yet, it feels so natural, so right to do so. Never have I felt so appealing, so glorious, so human. Yet, here I am, dripping cunt juice, desperate to lick the sperm off him. I want to cover myself in everything that is Adam. His smell, his breath, his cum.

I am rocked quickly back to reality by a shocking blow. Adam has backhanded me across my face. He is slapping my breasts, whacking my ass, and backhanding my face. I am in such shock, I don't even recoil. What? Why?

I rally and cry out. This just seems to spur him on. He hits me harder. It's so intense that I begin to sob. I pull my legs into the fetal position, attempting to shield what I can and endure what I cannot. Still, Adam continues.

I am now sobbing loudly, tears streaming down my face. I cry out, "How is this love?"

He stops suddenly. I say it again, "How is this love?"

Adam cocks his head to one side, as though he has never considered this question before.

"How is this love?"

He gathers me up in his arms and holds me close. He kisses my neck and wipes my tears. He says nothing. Not a fucking word. I sit in this space and have no idea what to make of it.

Finally, after what seems like an eternity, Adam says, "It is one thing to submit to me. It's another to feel your submission."

WHAT? What the fuck?

"Catherine, you submit out of pleasure. You don't submit out of devotion. At least, not yet. You need to feel what it is to totally and completely submit. This is a way of loving you don't yet know. It may not make sense to you, but I am completely and totally devoted to you."

I am incredulous. Surely, my face reveals this. He smiles gently and strokes my hair. "Catherine, my pet, I cherish you. Someday, you will cherish me."

But I DO! This is what I am feeling. I DO!

"Someday, you will gladly welcome a slap or a blow. Someday, you will doubt my love for you if it has been too long since I have disciplined you. Someday…", he trails off.

And I thought I was conflicted before today.

Shit. Fuck. Damn.

I am beside myself. What is this "devotion" Adam speaks of? I bristle a bit to his touch. He senses this and does the opposite of what I expect: he pulls me even closer. He whispers in my ear, "Catherine, you are mine. Catherine, Catherine, Catherine." This is like the balm for my wounds. I find myself unable to resist. I push against him so as much of his skin is in contact with mine. I close my eyes and allow myself to simply surrender to the moment.

Adam won't let me go. He holds me tightly and continues stroking my hair. My breathing slows and I feel I am drifting off. Some time passes and I wake to Adam gently applying arnica and cool packs to my red skin. He smiles at me. "I like taking care of you." *And yet you are the reason I need this care.*

"Adam, I still don't understand. If you like taking care of me, why would you hit me?"

"Catherine, I don't owe you an explanation. As a sub, you are simply to obey. Do you understand that? But you are exceptional to me, very special. My job is to train you, to shape you. As a submissive, your job is to anticipate my needs and to meet them. Further, in doing so, you should find fulfillment. This is the piece that is missing. I am devoted to your training. You are not yet devoted to me."

"But I do find fulfillment…" my voice trails off.

"No, Catherine, you find pleasure."

There was no denying that. I had never experienced such pleasure before. I hadn't considered this shift in stance from deriving pleasure from stimulation versus deriving pleasure from meeting someone's else's needs.

"You are right," I hear myself saying, "I don't know what it means to find pleasure or fulfillment in meeting someone else's needs. You are right."

Adam smiles. "Yes, Catherine. I am glad you see that. You have a ways to go. I will be patient with you to a point, but I will push you, if that's what's required." And with that he swept me up in his arms and carried me to the shower. He placed me on a marble bench and began to wash my body. I put up my hand. He paused.

"Adam, let me start here, here in this moment." I stood up, motioned gently for him to sit down, and I set about to wash his body in the most loving way I knew how. And thus began, for real, my training.

So, what does it mean to serve someone? How does a person derive satisfaction and joy from caring for someone else? These questions were swirling in my head. Honestly, in my life, I had been so focused on myself, I had not considered these before. And honestly, I had never cared to consider this. Everyone in my life served me, from my exceptionally competent house manager to the custodian who cleaned my office at Bolton Financial. Here I was, about to lay all that aside, and devote myself utterly and completely to another.

I left the House of S resolved to learn to serve Adam. I was determined to prove to him I could do this, and not just COULD do this, but would willingly and happily do this. I wasn't sure of my motivation, but I was sure I was committed. Adam made me feel different than anyone I had ever known and I was prepared to risk a lot to grow the connection that was emerging. I mean, when he looked at me, I got wet. When he said my name, I came close to orgasm. When he touched my hair, I swooned. When he looked at me, I blushed with pride and desire.

The next week I managed to be my effective self at work. I poured myself into every task. It was as if by committing to Adam, I no longer was insecure about what was to come. I trusted him. I now believed him. He enjoyed caring for me, training me. I was his beloved pet. When I looked in the mirror, I felt like a fancy parrot, preening in preparation of seeing her mate.

On Wednesday, I met with S in the comfort of her office. She greeted me, smiling warmly, dressed in a 1920's vintage satin dressing gown. In my business suit and heels, I thought how glorious it would be to wear such exotic clothing to work. She rang a buzzer and her masseur entered.

"I thought you might like a foot rub today. I can't imagine spending a work day in those heels." S pointed him in the right direction and soon I was sitting back, eyes half closed as he massaged my feet and ankles.
"Catherine, I believe you have found a new resolve. I even see it in how you carry yourself."

I open my eyes, wishing for just a few more minutes of peace, but I respond nonetheless: "S, I am beginning to understand what my task is. I realized last week that I have never devoted myself to another. I might have done this if I had a child, but I am not fully sure that even then it would be complete devotion of the heart. I mean, I imagine I would spare no expense for my offspring, but I see that is different than being devoted. I want to know what this is, this devotion to another."

"Catherine, that is the beginning of the great awakening. You have the desire. Now, you have to learn what it really means. You will have to live it. That's why I am proposing you commit to seven days, seven days with Adam and no one else. No phone calls, no emails, no work, just Adam. Is that something you can manage? And before you answer, consider how many vacations you have actually taken in your life. Why do you deprive yourself of the joy and restoration such time away allows?"

She was right. I was indeed a slave to Bolton Financial. My employees did as I directed. Still, I was required to be there. It was a tether, an anchor. I was in no way free.

I was surprised at my response. "S, I will find a way. I want to do this while my resolve is strong."

"Well, then, Catherine. I propose one full week, beginning this Saturday. I have a cabin about 100 miles from here. It's remote but very comfortable. There's no WiFi. No phone. You will have the space you need to begin a journey of devotion. Now, before you think of all the reasons why this is too soon, just now, it will always be too soon and also not soon enough…"

S knew how to play me. Also not soon enough was enough of a challenge for me to take the bait and say yes. I spent the next two days meeting with managers and my personal assistant to make sure there was a clear plan for the following week. Bolton Financial would march ahead as always, even with the head 100 miles away and for all intents and purposes, unreachable.

S sent a car to pick me up Friday evening. The driver took my bag and opened the door. There, in the back seat of the plush sedan was Adam. I simply melted. I slid in under his welcoming arm and rested my head against his shoulder. "Catherine, you are mine. You know this, right?" I gave a small nod and snuggled in even closer. The time passed quickly. Adam kept me next to him the entire way. He had me curl up with my head in his lap, his erection a welcome cushion. He played with my hair and occasionally slipped his hands down to circle and caress my tits. My cunt ached, ached for him.

We arrived 90 minutes later. The cabin's lights were on. Clearly, S had sent a team to attend to every detail.

Adam swept me up into his arms and carried me in like a bride, setting me down on an oversized leather armchair with comfy ottoman. A smiling man in a chef's coat poked his head around the corner and said, "Sir, dinner is warm and in the oven. I will deliver breakfast when you ring me in the morning. Good night, sir. Good night, ma'am." And with that, we were alone.

Adam turned to me with a serious look on his face. Catherine, take off your clothes, all of them, and put on the harness that's in the bathroom. That is all you will wear for the next week." I must have paused a bit too long and I saw his response too late. He was on me with a torrent of slaps. He grabbed my chin and held my head so our eyes met. "Catherine, is this how you show your devotion?"

I attempted to shake my head no, but his grasp was too firm. I mumbled, "No," and then quickly added, "sir."

"Now that's a good girl. Be quick." I scrambled out of the chair, my face still smarting from the slaps. The bathroom was off the bedroom. It was rather luxurious for a cabin with a separate claw-footed tub, a stand-alone double shower with multiple sprays and a massive rainwater shower head in the center. There was a bidet and a toilet in small closed off closet-sized space and then double sinks and a large vanity. The walls were essentially covered in mirrors, though not so much as to create the dizzying illusion of infinity. Hanging on a satin covered hanger was a one-piece red leather harness. I pulled off my clothes and neatly folded them. I peed then gave myself a good wash with the bidet and stepped into the harness. This last act had an immediate impact on me. I was no longer Catherine Standish Bolton, founder and CEO of Bolton Financial, a role I was most comfortable with. Instead, I was Adam's pet, here to do his bidding and bring him pleasure, and I questioned my ability to do this nearly as well.

The driver must have partially unpacked my bag because my toiletries and cosmetics are on the vanity. I grab my perfume, a heady mix of jasmine, sandalwood, and mogra purchased on a trip to Asia years back. I put on lipstick and pull my hair up into a ponytail. I step out and head to the living area to present myself to Adam. I hope he is pleased. He is sitting in the comfortable leather chair. He motions for me to turn around slowly. As my back turns toward him I feel a yank. He has grabbed the harness and I stumble backwards into his lap. He is strong enough to slow down my fall, but I remain mentally off balance. I tell myself, *you chose this*. Is this positive self-talk or recrimination?

I am still facing backwards. Adam spreads my legs apart and places my arms on the arms of the chair. He begins fondling my breasts. He goes for a "temperature check" with his hand spreading my labia and looking for telltale signs of welcome. I am so attuned to his touch at this point, that pearl-colored liquid is plentiful and beginning to seep out. "Ah, good, my pet. This is how I like you."

Suddenly, he sits me up and pushes me off his lap. But, instead of allowing me to stand, he forces me down onto my knees. "Unzip my pants." I do as I am told, his cock pushing against my hands the entire time. "Suck on me." I free his penis and begin sliding my mouth up and down. It's already fully erect and I struggle to take it deeply into my mouth. He allows me to adjust to the side, on my feet but bent over, in order to elongate my throat. I swear his erection is even harder than usual. The head is so swollen that the skin gleams in the light, it is stretched so tightly. I wonder if he will cum in my mouth.

Adam grabs my ponytail and pulls my head up. "Stand up". I do. He walks me into the bedroom where there is a massive four poster bed. I hadn't noticed during my rush to the bathroom, but the posts have sturdy round metal rings attached. What looks decorative has a clear purpose. Adam quickly attaches cuffs to my wrists and then the cuffs to leather leashes attached to the rings. He kicks my legs apart. My heartbeat quickens. I am both afraid and excited, what a heady mix.

He pulls my hips back toward him. I hear the foil wrapper of a condom tearing open. Adam's pants unceremoniously drop to the floor and he steps out of them. His cock is rubbing between my legs getting coated in pearly cunt juice. When he slides past my clit I moan. Suddenly, he thrusts inside me hard and fast. I gasp at the sensation. His right hand wraps around to my clit and he begins to rub it mercilessly. He uses his left hand to stabilize my hips. He pounds me with a fury I've never experienced. He senses I am close and he quickens his pace ever so slightly. In a moment, I feel his cock pulsing and my legs weaken as I cum. He makes one last hard push and then wraps his arms around me and lays his chest against my back.

I am expecting him to unclip me so we can cuddle. Instead, he pulls out and heads to the bathroom, his shirt and socks still on. A few minutes later he returns with just a towel wrapped around his waist and a small cat o'nine tails in his hand. He has no intention of releasing me. In fact, he bends down to attach cuffs to my ankles and tethers me to the bed frame. He runs his hand between my legs and brings it up to my face.

"Lick my hand. I want you to taste what you taste like." Strangely, I am not horrified at this idea. His hand smells of sea water and glistens slightly. I extend my tongue and the taste is mildly salty. Adam steps back and begins to whip me lightly. The sensation is mildly stimulating. My body now associates this with foreplay, as I feel my labia swelling. He begins to deepen the strikes and the blood rises to the surface of my skin. He pauses and presses his body next to mine, reaching around to pull and twirl my nipples. Cunt juice starts to run down my leg. He takes note and smiles.

He rearranges my hand leashes so now my arms are together above my head, my legs still apart. He dips his hand into my vagina and then massages my asshole with the slippery pearl essence. He drops the towel and rubs his cock between my legs. He is already hard and getting harder. Again I hear the sound of a condom wrapper. Adam comes back to coating his condom-covered penis with my juice and then he presses against my ass. The head slides in slowly. He pauses to allow my body to relax and then begins to masterfully fuck me in the ass. Adams uses both hands to stimulate me. One is pulling the labia wide open. The other is moving between clit and cunt, stroking, circling, penetrating. I begin a series of orgasms that are other-worldly. He is more gentle with my ass, but his persistent movement is only becoming more intense. I reach another peak and as my vagina quivers in a spasm of gripping and releasing, he pushes in deeply and I feel his orgasm. He holds himself still and I feel every pulsing contraction. It is the most intimate thing I have ever experienced.

Again, he leaves me bound to the bed frame as he cleans up. I hear the sound of the bathtub filling. Some minutes later, Adam emerges and finally unclips me, removing the cuffs. He slides me out of the harness and takes my hand. He lets me relieve myself but insists the door stay open. My clit is still a swollen sphere as I push the urine past it, I have another orgasm. He takes this in.

The tub is quite large. The taps are in the middle above the tub in the wall to the back. He helps me into the warm foamy water. It smells of lavender. He slips into the other end. We are facing each other. He changes his mind and has me turn so my back is to him. He lays me back against his body and we remain like this for minutes on end. The water cools, so Adam sits me up and turns the hot water tap on. Again, we lay back and soak. My eyes close and I drift off for a bit to the sound of the water trickling in. I wake to Adam moving me again. He steps out of the tub first. I realize in that moment what I should do, and I quickly join him. While I am dripping wet, I grab a large towel from the warming bar and begin to dry him off. He cocks his head and smiles at me. I feel my heart leap in my chest. I have earned his approval. I wrap him in a waffle-weave robe and slide pristine slippers onto his feet. "Sir, may I dry myself please?"

His grin grows broader. "Yes, Catherine. That would be fine. When you finish, join me in the living room."

"Yes, sir." I set about getting myself sorted quickly. I even manage to brush my hair. I start to put on a robe and have second thoughts. Instead, I find the halter and slide back into it.

Adam has set out dinner at the table. There's a bottle of champagne in a chrome bucket, too. The moment feels celebratory. I approach, tucking my chin in a bit and lowering my eyes. "Sir, what can I do to help?"

"At this moment, Catherine, nothing. You are doing so well today. Let us celebrate your progress." And with that he pops the cork on the bottle.

The meal is delicious. I feel like I have never eaten food before. Tender baby beets with butter and parsley, a fillet butterflied over mashed Japanese sweet potato with a garlic herb red wine reduction, snow peas with a touch of ginger and sesame oil. The champagne is Veuve Clicquot La Grande Dame. I find the title ironic until I consider this is perhaps a nod to S herself.

Adam seems relaxed and sweet. I catch myself becoming self-absorbed and I put my focus back on him. Instead of dominating or directing the conversation, I listen and ask questions. I am surprised how much I enjoy simply hearing him talk. His voice has a quality that is deep and slightly hoarse with honey overtones. He could be talking about the weather and I would be in rapture.

As we finish eating, I ask him if I might rub his back. He cocks his head in that way that indicates he is both surprised and pleased. "Why yes, Catherine, that would be lovely." We move to the bed. I pull back the duvet and help him out of the robe. I go to the bathroom, certain I will find what I need, and sure enough, in the cupboard there is an assortment of massage oils. I smell several and settle on the one with citrus overtones with a touch of ylang ylang.

I allow the oil to drizzle out of the bottle into the depression on either side of his backbone. I straddle his ass and push my palms up, along his spine, out from his neck to his shoulders, and then down along his sides. His skin feels amazing. I appreciate that I have time and space to begin to know the contours of his body.

I move to sit lower down on his hamstrings and massage his gorgeous ass. There is this lovely dishing in where the gluteus medius meets the gluteus maximus. I love how hard his muscles feel under his smooth, polished skin. I find myself kissing his tailbone and tracing my fingers down between his checks. I put more massage oil on my fingers and go in search of his asshole. I tease him by circling the outside and massaging the perineum. Gently, I press one finger and then two moving in and out of his ass. I massage the back of his prostate from the inside and an audible moan leaves his lips. Bingo.

His body responds with another erection. I step into the bathroom to wash my hands. He follows behind me, glorious and naked. He holds me from behind and presses his hard cock into the small of my back. I reach back to touch his face. I look in the mirror and love what I see. He caresses my breasts and kisses my neck. He picks me up in his arms, carries me to the bed, and buries his face between my legs. Soon, we are a mass of arms, legs, moans, and passion. I had no idea sex could be like this.

I wake to the sound of birds. It's the hour right before dawn when the birds wake up. Cacophony in the dark. Adam is spooning me, his right arm draped over my side. The harness isn't on. I don't even recall when it came off. I think about the last twelve hours. It feels like a lifetime. It's day one of seven and I am already over-the-moon. I close my eyes and drift off again, imagining I am in the tub of warm water, laying back against Adam's chest.

We officially wake up around 9. Adam calls the chef who comes and prepares an elegant breakfast -- French toast made with croissant, topped with fresh berries and a drizzle of maple syrup, parmesan and asparagus omelets, and the perfect French Press coffee. I am allowed to wear a robe over my harness. We are like honeymooners with a deep dark secret. A maid replaces the towels, changes the sheets, and tidies up. The chef leaves a cold lunch in the fridge and he and the maid depart.

Adam tells me he wants to give me a special treat today. My heart leaps wondering what more could happen. He instructs me to take off the harness and go sit on the floor of the shower. I dutifully follow instructions. He comes in completely naked. I am envisioning sex in the shower. He tells me to close my eyes and open my mouth. Hmmm. I am expecting his cock to rub against my lips. I feel a warm stream of liquid on the top of my head, my face, my chest and shoulders, and then in my mouth. It's a bit salty. I open my eyes to see Adam pissing on me. My eyes widen. He laughs. "Silly. I told you to keep your eyes shut." He smacks my face and continues peeing on me. I try to disassociate a bit. When I do this, his urine feels warm and not yucky. I put out my tongue to taste it again. Salty and a bit acidic. I bring my hands up to form a cup and catch as much of it as I can. I smell it, dip my tongue in it, and then pour it over my head. Adam laughs. "Oh Catherine, you are a delight. You are a very special pet indeed. Maybe, some day, I will taste your piss."

He turns on the shower and selects the option for the side multi-sprays. We are awash in pulsing water. His hands are all over me, slipping in and out of my cunt and my ass. He grabs soap and I take it from him with a smile. I wash his body like it's the most precious object I am entrusted with. I spend time running my soapy, slippery hand down his butt crack to his balls. This gives rise to a luscious erection. I dive in with my mouth, cupping his balls with my hands. He begins to pump in and out, fucking my mouth. I push my chin down so I can take in more of him. He looks down. Our eyes meet. He closes his and gives in completely to the motion, in and out, in and out, in and out. He pulls out as he is cumming and sprays my face. I catch as much as I can with my tongue. He is glorious and I adore him.

I dry him off. He puts the harness back on me and tugs me to the bed. He puts me over his legs and proceeds to spank me till my ass is glowing red. He then covers it with kisses and runs his tongue teasingly toward my ass. He pulls me up onto my knees and gently pulls my cheeks apart. He moves his tongue in circles around my asshole and then presses the full length of his tongue against it. I am a mess, moaning and begging to be fucked. His fingers find their way to my wet cunt, and he rolls me over and massages the uppermost edge back and forth. My body responds with a gush of secretions from every gland. I am sure there is a puddle on the bed. He smiles approvingly, "That's my girl," he says as he unrolls a condom. He pulls me to the end of the bed and secures cuffs to my ankles, tethering them high. My ass hangs just off the bed. I am wide open, vulnerable, and completely at his mercy. He fucks me long and hard, making me cum over and over.

We eat lunch late. A simpler repast - smoked salmon, rye crisps, and caviar, sour cream, and a selection of accoutrements --

chopped hard-boiled egg, spring onion, and a particularly yummy chopped dill pickle. Dom Perignon was the perfect foil. Dessert was creme brulee with fresh raspberries and a sweet dessert wine from California -- a Wild Horse viognier.

Adam tells me to get dressed to go for a walk. I pull on mom jeans, sneakers, and a t-shirt over my harness. It feels a bit saucy to know what I am wearing underneath my street clothes!

We head out into the woods while the chef and maid step in to make things perfect for our return.

"Pet, for this walk, I want you beside me at all times." I slide up next to him. He takes my hand and we walk in silence. I have never felt that I belonged so much. I realize this sounds completely crazy. I do not even know his last name. Yet, I feel closer to this man than anyone I have ever known.

The air is warming. Spring is turning to summer. What a perfect metaphor for the moment. I find myself feeling happier and more settled than I can remember. I belong to him. I am secure in this knowledge.

Adam must sense my thoughts. He stops and pulls me close, pressing my cheek against his chest, he holds me close. "It's strange, isn't it? To be so close to someone in the present and yet know nothing of their past and their future. It's a thing of beauty, really. It's almost Zen-like. And Catherine, I want you to know what a privilege it is to train you. I find you desirable and delightful. My motivation isn't just that this is what I am to do - it's that I am passionate about doing it. I hope you feel that passion."

Feel it? Fuck, yay! MORE than feel it. I am more alive than I can remember...ever. My struggle is in finding a label, a way to categorize this experience. Again, Adam must be reading my mind.

"Catherine, there is no label for this. That is its beauty. We find ourselves in serving another. I serve you by training you. You serve me by showing and then living your devotion. It is special. A label would limit it. There should be no limit. Give yourself to me without reservation."

I wonder how I would give myself beyond what I have. I see that life has been a zero-sum game for me to this point. I win. You lose. I haven't known the I win/you win paradigm.

We continue walking till we reach a stream. Adam sits against a large granite boulder and pulls me in toward him. I don't even find his positioning of me strange. It's a peculiar and powerful comfort that this gorgeous human wants me next to him. He surrounds me with his arms and we just rest here, breathing, for some time.

I feel peaceful. How often do I spend time -- any time ever -- NOT making decisions? I cannot even remember a time when I relinquished control. And yet, how freeing was it to simply let go and let him determine what, when, where, and how. I smile, thinking there will be more surprises around the corner. Bring it.

We head back and I feel ten years younger. I hunger for what's next. Adam has energy in his strides. It's the honeymoon I never had.

When we reach the cabin, it is spotless. There's a yummy smell in the air -- dinner in the warming oven. Adam, sits in the comfy leather chair and pulls me into his lap. He is all kisses and caresses, though I feel his cock waking up and pressing against my legs and ass. He slips my shirt off and explores my chest. I lay my head back and take it all in. The alternate sucking and twirling of my nipples between thumb and index finger triggers a reaction between my legs. I, too, am waking up.

He carries me to the bed, unbuttoning and sliding my mom jeans off. He stands back and looks at me. "Catherine, you are glorious." And with that, he begins making love to me. I feel beloved, cherished, adored. Each orgasm is a higher high. I realize that his excitement for me is fueling something deep within. I am changing how I see myself. I am no longer just the doer. I am the receiver, too. And I am worthy of this.

The week progresses from one high to the next. I find myself excited to feel his hand on me, whether it is a slap, a spanking, or a caress. We are constantly entwined...in the bed, in the bath, in the chair. I begin to know when he is close to cumming and I take delight in pushing him over the edge. I wrap my ankles with my legs up over his back and pull him down close, pressing him against my pubic bone. As he feels my vagina quiver with yet another orgasm, he succumbs himself. When he is behind me, I tilt my pelvis, narrowing the hymen. If he is fucking me in the ass, I relax to let him slide all the way in and out. If he is letting me suck on him, my fingers are massaging his perineum or his ass. I am beginning to know his body intimately, just like he knows mine.

Each day unfolds another dream. Adam surprises me with sensual play. He blindfolds me and ties me to the bed facedown, legs and arms apart. He begins teasing me by dripping warm wax on my lower back and buttocks. He coats toys in warm coconut. He inserts a butt plug and then remotely controls its levels of vibration. He then inserts a narrow vibrator into my vagina and presses it up against my g-spot. As if that isn't enough, the same device has a curved exterior piece that reaches up and presses against my clit.

Adam delights in making me shudder, moan, and beg for him to fuck me as he brings me to the edge over and over. He unclips me and rolls me over, leaving the maddening vibrating butt plug in place. He puts on a condom, smiles, and then dives in. My vagina is narrowed a bit due to the rather wide plug. This heightens the sensation for both of us. He has held me at the height of arousal for some time and I cum quickly, shaking from head to toe. He pauses briefly and then begins again. I whisper, "I want you," into his ear. He complies and cums. I feel every single contraction and the crazy vibrations of the butt plug. I press hard against him and rub my clit side to side, bringing myself to yet another climax even as he lays nearly motionless.

There are walks, dinners, baths, massages, and connection. I am beginning to feel like I am an extension of Adam or he is an extension of me. I certainly feel this physically. He exercises free rein over my body and I know him intimately as well. I feel comfortable in my nakedness, even as someone at least ten years older. He looks at me in a way that communicates I am desirable. He doesn't want me because I can do him a favor, give him a job, or launch his company. He doesn't want me for my impeccable reputation, my managerial skills, or my ambition. He does, however, want me. He wants me because I want him. He wants me because I submit to his desires. He wants me because my focus, my attention is on him. He demands this, and I willingly comply.

What this means for me, I am not at all sure I know. I do know that when I am with him, I am very much in the present moment. Something as simple as a blindfold heightens my other senses. In the middle of the unknown, I am drawn in deeper and deeper.

I also know how safe I feel to be completely vulnerable and open with him. And intimate beyond any intimacy I've experienced. And no shame, no embarrassment. My ass is as desirable as my mouth. Cunt juice streaming down my leg is a badge of honor not something to apologize for. I realize it is Adam who has made this possible.

But what we have is very much dependent on the well-orchestrated backdrop, the stage set. The cabin is a fantasy. I will be going back to the office in a few days where I will once again be the master of that domain. I wonder if I will feel any different or I will simply slip back into the role I have so artfully created for myself.

On the last evening after yet another round of sexual play, I find myself becoming anxious about leaving this bubble. Adam senses the shift and responds so sweetly. He draws a bath and uncorks a bottle of blanc de noir champagne, the pink color the result of the juice of black grapes. He settles me in the bath with a glass and fetches a small table to hold the champagne bucket. As he slides in behind me, I take another sip, swallow, and then find my voice, "Adam, I mean, sir." He smiles at my slip. "Sir, what happens when we return? What I mean is this has been so incredible and it's also unsustainable. I don't want it to end, but I know it will all too soon."

"My dear Catherine, you must know S anticipates every concern."

"Yes, of course. Of course, she does, but do you know what will happen next? And can you share that with me?"

"Well, I don't actually know what's ahead. I do know that S will have given this a great deal of thought and she will have a plan. I do suspect there will be a plan to support you through the sub-drop."

"The sub-drop?"

"Yes, Catherine, you have already experienced this. It's when the endorphin levels return to normal after the incredible rush of intense connections. It can feel draining, depressing even. At any rate, I know S will have a plan for you so the drop isn't a crash landing."

I consider this. I imagine my endorphin levels have been through the roof all week. It's been one high after the other. I suddenly imagine sleeping alone without Adam there and tears begin to stream down my cheeks.

Adam responds by pulling me closer. He takes my glass and sets it next to his on the small table next to the champagne bucket. He envelopes me in his arms and then he begins to gently stroke my hair. I give into the feelings and the gentle stream becomes a torrent.

Finally, when I have cried it all out, Adam turns me around to face him. "Catherine, have you ever wondered what it means to fall in love with yourself?"

His question feels like it's coming from left field. I mean, what does loving myself have to do with this?

"Catherine, sometimes when we are with someone we really like, someone who is really focused on us, we can think we are in love with that person, when, in fact, we are in love with the attention. When someone focuses on us so single mindedly it might be the first time since we were helpless infants that our world revolved so closely around our needs, our desires. If you step back for just a moment, and instead of focusing on what's coming at you, focus on what's happening inside you, I think you might see things from a different perspective."

"And what perspective is that?" my voice, a strange mix of bitterness, cynicism, and curiosity.

"What are words you would use to describe how you have felt this week? Limit yourself to just five words that would encompass how you have felt."

Huge pause. I consider the stream of words that my brain is happily spewing: elated, cherished, ecstatic, sensual, connected, excited, ageless, delighted, overwhelmed, cared for, capable, desired, elegant, exposed, celebratory, at ease…I realize that loved and loving aren't on the list. Interesting. Okay, hmmm, now to pick five words. I choose cherished, sensual, ageless, desired, and connected.

"And now, from this list of five, pick only three."

Another pause...Round two, I choose connected, cherished, and ageless.

Adam, nods. "All right, now, select just one, just one of the words, the one that best describes how you feel."

Wow. It's a real toss-up between connected and cherished.

"Cherished, I feel cherished." I look for his reaction and his face seems unreadable.

"Catherine, I do cherish you. You are worthy of my attention. You are worthy like only a prized pet can be. I have something for you. I'd like to give it to you at dinner."

Dinner is yet another thoughtfully planned meal -- chicken breast in a white wine, butter, and roasted garlic sauce over green fettuccine with caramelized baby carrots in a rainbow of hues to balance the color on the plate. Dessert is a pungent creamy Rouge et Noir Schloss cheese with toasted rounds of a nut and seed dark bread with slices of red pear. It's the most sensual of desserts we've had, a range of flavors and textures to rival the range of activities in the adjacent bedroom. Instead of champagne, a yummy full-flavored Sauvignon Blanc is perfect with dinner and holds its own against the aroma and pungency of the cheese.

Adam pulls out a simple white box tied with a red satin ribbon. "Catherine, I have something for you." And with that, he puts the box in my hands. For some silly reason, I shake it the way a child sometimes shakes wrapped presents under the Christmas Tree, hoping the sound will reveal some important clue about the contents. I tug at the ribbon and lift the lid. Peeling back the tissue paper, there is a polished steel necklace of sorts, a circle with a smaller circle in the front. I realize what this is now. I raise my eyes to look into his.

"Catherine, I want you to wear this 24 hours a day, every day, no matter what. When the time comes, and you will know if and when that is, you may remove it. He stands behind me and opens the necklace which divides into two perfect half circles and then he unites the ends of the choker again. He fishes in the tissue paper until his fingers find a small key. I hear a click. With that, the choker is secure.

"Come." He walks me to the bathroom and removes my kimono. I stand in front of a full-length mirror, naked but for the harness and the collar, the perfect pet.

Re-entry is a confusing mix of feelings. I am relieved to be back in familiar territory. I am incredibly sad to be parting. Adam is unbelievably sweet. He helps get my bag upstairs. He closes the bedroom door, clearly aware of the need for discretion, before he comes and holds me against his chest for what feels like minutes. He strokes my hair. Finally, he lifts my chin so our eyes meet. "Catherine, you are amazing. It is a joy to be your master. S will be sending along some things to help you re-integrate. I will see you soon, my pet." And with that, he is gone.

My house manager appears and senses the mood. "Catherine, let me have the chef bring a tray up for lunch. What else might I do for you?" I shake my head. I have no clue what anyone can do for me at this point.

On the lunch tray is an embossed note with S's signature initial. I sigh and then open it. I am not sure I can take any more surprises or experiences right now.

Catherine,

I am certain you feel a bit lost right now. It's to be expected. It's hard to come down from such intense experiences. I do know how this feels. My masseur is coming over in about 30 minutes. Please let him set up a table and work on you. This will help.

S

As promised, I am soon laid out on a massage table, being stroked and rubbed with lavender and ylang ylang scented oils. Before the masseur finishes, he begins to fill the bathtub with the same smelling bubble bath that was at the cabin. He instructs me to soak for at least thirty minutes and then to crawl into bed and sleep until I wake up naturally. I know enough by now to do as I am told.

So, the week follows with daily treats from S. There's a basket with the Schloss cheese and red pears, along with the Sauvignon Blanc from the last night at the cabin. Another one appears with an incredible selection of dark chocolate truffles, including red chile infused ones. A bottle of dessert wine is tucked in. The masseur stops by every evening, offering a head massage, a foot rub, or a full-on massage. I feel odd at first accepting all this attention, but I say yes to each offering and I feel more balanced as each day goes by. S sends notes every day. I feel cared for, cherished, and it feels good.

I decide I need to meet with Brad to process these events. I want an external viewpoint on what I hope is progress. My assistant sets up the meeting for Wednesday. I manage to step back into my role as CEO of Bolton Financial like I would fresh from a vacation. I am surprised I have energy for work, but luckily, I do. There are a few IPO's to analyze and some short sales that might prove profitable. My staff have done a remarkable job in my absence. I make sure they know that I know this.

I step into Brad's waiting room feeling a bit raw. How much do I want to reveal? I feel especially vulnerable.

"Catherine, so good to see you. Come in. I want to hear how it's going."

"Brad, I think I have made a shift of sorts, but I am not totally sure of where this new perspective leads. I've jotted some notes. May I share?" He nods.

"When I came to you six months ago, I felt dissatisfied with life. I have, by all external measures, achieved a great deal of success, but I felt empty, hollow. You advised me to pursue a rather novel course of inquiry, facilitated by S. While the events have been surprising, even shocking, I feel I have managed well up to this point." I pause there and look up. Brad tilts his head slightly, his interest piqued.

"In the course of this journey," I note I am using S's favorite word, "I have spent significant time with one person, my dom. His name is Adam. He recently said something I am working to make sense of. He spoke of falling in love with oneself." I pause here, hoping Brad will pick up the thread.

"And?" Hmmm, an invitation to continue, but what to say?

"Well, here's what I have in my notes. These are my observations:

- I have been able to sustain being in the moment for progressively longer periods of time. In fact, at times, I have no sense of time. I am that much in the now.
- I have opened myself up to another human in ways I have never done before.
- I feel no shame, only joy and celebration, with my body.
- I have never felt this attended to, even by the numerous people in my world who want to curry my favor.
- I have never focused on another person so intently before in my life.
- I have never trusted anyone so much as I trust Adam.
- I enjoy bringing pleasure to someone else.

I pause and look up, "So what do you make of my observations?"

"Catherine, it seems in some ways you've met one of your goals, which was to live, not just have a life. It sounds like you are truly living, at least for part of the time. Wouldn't you agree?"

I nod.

He continues, "How does food taste to you?" *What kind of crazy question is that*, I wonder. I mean, seriously, what does food have to do with *this*?

He repeats the question: "Catherine, how does food taste to you now?"

I suppress a desire to roll my eyes. I do sit back in my chair, take a breath, and consider how to answer this. In this space, Brad dives in again, "Catherine, after one of your experiences with Adam, how does food taste?"

I think of the meals in the cabin. I could recite every single item we ate. I could likely tell you the seasoning used. I certainly remember the wine pairings.

Then I think of my five Saturdays. Each time when I returned home I was starving, ravenous.

"And how about, smell, Catherine? How is your sense of smell?"

I am beginning to piece things together. S sent over a bouquet that mimicked the smells in her bouquet. The masseur used the same bubble bath as the one at the cabin. Even his massage oil matched.

"Yes, Brad, I think these have shifted. I definitely have had more of an appetite and I think I have really savored food, perhaps more than I ever have. And I do think I am noticing smells more than before. Some even carry memories for me."

"Your senses are heightened, wouldn't you say?" *Yes, I would. I should have added this to my observations.*

"And why do you think this is so?" Well, THAT'S a million-dollar question…

"I guess part of this is just being more present to what's happening. I also think that as I experience new things, I feel this excitement, like the excitement of discovery, and somehow that drives my appetite. Like afterwards, I really, truly, am hungry! But Brad, there's a deeper hunger, I'm afraid. One that is below the superficial. I totally acknowledge I am living much more now. And yet, I know there is more to it. I just don't know what to do to move from point 1a to b."

"Catherine, you have to realize that you spent most of your life driven by one goal, building Bolton Financial. And you have done a masterful job of building that company. Seriously, so many of my clients would totally envy where you are now. But your laser-like focus has meant so much of life has been excluded, passed over, or ignored. You are retraining yourself to pay attention to what's happening now. How is being more present affecting you?"

I consider this question seriously. What has changed?

"Brad, I am not sure where to begin. I guess my question is, is all this necessary? I mean, this has been a very intense process. Was this required?"

"I read a meme today. Sometimes, these seem over-simplified statements, but this one stood out as true to me: *Stop holding yourself back. If you don't like where you are, make a change.* You have to recognize that you wouldn't have gotten to this place without a rather dramatic change in your world. If I had told you that you needed to be more present in the moment, how would you have achieved that? If I had said that the first step is to savor something as simple as each bite of food, would you have made a change in order to experience that? Would you have dutifully gone home and eaten each bite mindfully, chewing each morsel 20 times, reflecting on the journey the food made to get to your plate? I think not. When we, as humans, are longing for change, we rarely have the willpower or means to get there. The journey you are taking is throwing you off balance just enough that you have the possibility of change. Do you see that?"

"I agree. I wouldn't have been able to shift much on my own. Still…"

"Catherine, you have to recognize that you have approached things a certain way for a long period of time, more than 40 years, I would say. And that means change will come in fits and starts. There will be sudden bursts of change that feel effortless and then there will be incremental change that feels painfully slow. One thing I know with certainty, and there isn't much in the world that I feel I am truly certain about, is that the only way a person can change is through direct experience that is novel and challenges the status quo profoundly. Everything else that is comfortable doesn't push a person hard enough to have any lasting impact."

He sat back, putting his lips together and with a slight shrug communicated that the ball was in my court. It was up to me. It had always been. All right then, S work your magic. I say, bring it.

Saturday rolls around and I find myself feeling excited about seeing Adam. I worry that the feeling isn't fully mutual. I am a bit older, and I know I am not his only "client." I consider the nature of my insecurity. What does it say about me? I realize there are things in my life I am very confident about. I also realize I have spent most of my life operating in the "more-than-confident-about" zone. I have been operating in a virtuous cycle where each success breeds more success. Is that a reason to shy away from the realm of countless things I am less than confident with? What am I afraid of? I step back and realize once again that this journey (there's that word again) is about so much more than sex.

As the heavy wooden door swings open and I step once again into the House of S, I pause and take in the smell. I note the hint of ylang ylang over a heady mix of rose, sandalwood, and mogra. It is not female nor male in nature but it is most definitely about passion and sensuality.

S is not in sight but my usual assistant is there, smiling. She ushers me to an oversized room on the top floor. "Catherine, S has planned something special today. I have hung your clothing options here for you. Please, for now, get comfortable and have a glass of champagne. Adam will be in shortly." She artfully pours the sparkling wine, a north coast Schramsberg, into a gorgeous glass and sets it on the small side table next to a boudoir-style armless chair.

How strange. I have never been given the option to select what I wear. Hmmm. What does this small change mean? I consider the options as I settle into the chair and sip the yummy brew, luscious with heady notes of lemon, pear, and almond. Damn, S has good taste.

After a few minutes -- time enough for me to have enjoyed a full glass and begun working on my second -- Adam comes in. Reflexively I stand, head down. He walks over, each footstep on the wood floor marking a rising warmth in my crotch. He lifts my chin so our eyes meet. He takes the glass from my hand and pulls me in close, kissing me passionately. I am grateful for this reunion.

Rather suddenly, he sits me back down in the chair and puts the glass in my hand. He pours himself a glass of the Schramsberg and pulls over a chair to sit close to me. "Catherine, today you will be with another person under my direction. I will be here the whole time, watching and directing. Your task is to please me by doing as I say."

I have heard his words but I am not fully sure what this means.

"The person you will be with is a male submissive. You will be in a dominant role with him but in submission to me."

I envision a corporate organizational chart. How ridiculous. This is nothing like that.

"Your first task is to select something to wear that will communicate your role -- dominant to him and submissive to me. Do you understand?"

I consider his instructions. Luckily, he is allowing me some time to process. There is no slap on the cheek in response to my pause. "Yes, I understand what I am to do, but I worry I won't carry out your intentions as you would want."

"Catherine, as long as you listen, you will do fine. If I am not directing you, you should do what feels right to you at that moment. I will correct you as needed. If you do a good job, I will reward you. If you don't, I won't. Now, you have five minutes to be ready." With that, Adam stood up and left.

I looked at the selection of clothing. There was the Barbarella outfit - nope -- too many connections to the slave auction. The teddy-thong was next. Okay, this could work, especially when compared with the harness and the thong. All right then, the teddy it is.

I decide to leave my hair down. I am not sure if this signals dominance but it is not the usual sub updo of the ponytail. I finish with a touch of power-red lipstick from my purse. At that exact moment, pursing my lips to spread the lipstick evenly, I spied the whip, a cat-o-nine-tails. Perfect. Whip in hand, I turn as the door opens. Adam ushers in a gorgeous smooth-skinned man dressed in a leather halter and thong. Wow. I am shocked at my reaction. The teddy is barely concealing the pearl-colored liquid leaking from my cunt.

He is something to behold: his smooth skin is coffee-with-cream colored, waxed, and slightly shiny, ridiculously fit with clean delineation of his muscles. His dark hair is pulled up into a man bun with side and back undercutting. It is all I can do to wait for instructions.

Adam sits in the boudoir chair and refills his glass. He looks at me. "Catherine, secure your sub to the bed frame, both ankles and wrists."

"Yes, sir." I approach the sub and when he doesn't move toward the bed, I give him a good smack in the right butt cheek with the whip. The way his skin flinches makes me even wetter.

"Move," I say, flashing my eyes. I attempt to channel my most authoritative voice and posture, securing him with the quick, tight pull of the cuffs. I smack his butt hard with my right hand, feeling the heat and tension of his glutes. I step forward, drawn in by his amazing body, cupping his cheeks and pressing my exposed breasts against his back below his shoulder blades. I hear Adam clear his throat and step back, turning to get instructions. He has tilted his chin to the right, lifting one eyebrow. Oh, my. I may have stepped out too soon.
"Catherine, warm him up. Use the whip to bring the blood to the surface."

I have NO experience doing this. I do know what it's like to be on the other side. I start somewhat tentatively, looking to see if the blows are meeting the objective. I look for his reflexive response, observing his pullback. Too much pullback means too much pain. Slight pullback means tolerable pain. I see his coffee-with-cream skin develop a pink undertone. I make sure to move to new targets after four or five blows, remembering that pain turns to tingles turns to numbness. The numbness leads to an "itch", an itch that wants more sensation.

After I work his backside, I unclip and reposition him facing me. He has the most gorgeous V-notch and I have to work to keep my eyes off his crotch. My goal is to warm him up and I am delighted to see the bulge in his g-string. I focus on his inner thighs, abdomen, and chest. I feel drawn to his nipples. I pause and suck hard on one, running my tongue over the tip and drawing it out, making it long, hard. He moans. I know I am meeting the mark.

I pull back and continue working on his skin, drawing my forearm slowly against his hard cock. More strikes on his thighs, then I cup and squeeze his balls with my left hand, pressing my breasts to his chest. I feel his body quiver. His eyes close and his head rolls back. Yes.

Adam speaks up, "Unclip him and make him lick you until you cum at least five times."

I unclip the sub and remove the cuffs. I grab his leash and pull him behind me. I lay back on the bed and push his head between my legs. He knows what he is doing and I cum quickly. I roll over and push my ass into the air. I push his head to my ass and I grab his right hand and place it on my clit. The sub presses his tongue in and circles my ass before he presses in and out of my asshole, matching the movement with this hand. Second orgasm, done. I sit up and pull on his harness, laying him out on the bed. I put my knees on either side of his head and sit down. The sub sucks on my clit and I fuck his face, moving my hips in small circles. I press down and rub hard. Oh my God, I cum hard. I decide to stay in this position, smearing pearl-colored cunt juice on his chin, mouth, and nose. I put his hands on my hips, and he gets the idea, moving me rhythmically, I cum long and hard.

I reposition the sub on his knees, my legs up over his shoulders, his hands supporting my calves. My butt is hanging over the edge of the bed with my ass and cunt fully exposed. The sub moves between the two zones, bouncing his head as though his head is his cock and hips. It isn't long before I am moaning and ridiculously wet. Fifth orgasm, done.

"Make him fuck you in the ass. Don't let him cum until I tell you."

I get a flash of inspiration. This will either be a great idea or an awful one, but I decide to go for it. I select a medium sized butt plug from the selection of toys next to the table. I dip it in the coconut oil. I tell him, "Take off your thong and bend over." He complies. I massage his ass with the plug, teasing him by pushing it slightly in and out. When I see his ass begin to relax, I push it in and out further until it slides in. "You will keep this in while you fuck me. I want your cock really hard." His liberated cock is already hard. I grab a condom and slide it over and then smear the warm coconut oil on his cock and balls. He responds. His penis rises up well past horizontal.

I decide to simply flip over and get on my knees. I take his cock in my hands and circle the head around my ass. I place it against my asshole and gently push back so that just the head is eased in. He understands and moves in and out slowly and gently. As I open up to him, he presses in deeper until he is buried inside me and fucking me hard. I grab his hand and put it on my clit. I tell him, "If you cum before I tell you, there will be a consequence. Do you understand?"

"Yes, ma'am." It's the first time I've heard his voice articulating words. It is luscious, sensual, and aroused. I reach around and smack his ass hard.

As I begin to cum, I sense he is close. I pause and smack his ass hard again. I repeat this until finally Adam gives the word. The sub and I cum together. It is overwhelming, the delay has made it all the more intense.

I realize that I have been working hard. My focus has been on the sub. I wonder if this is what it's like for Adam.

Adam speaks up, "Catherine, leave him. Crawl to me."

Crawl?... What?... Adam must sense my hesitation. His expression intensifies. I quickly snap to and get down. Rather than scoot across the floor, I decide to reach out with my right arm, head up, eyes on Adam. I let my body bend hard at the waist and I push my ass up in the air. I slither in the most sensuous way I can, a cross between a tiger slinking in the grass and the most sensuous slithering snake.

When I reach Adam, he pulls his thong to the side, his cock erect with a pearl of pre-cum glistening at the tip. He threads his hand through my hair, close to my scalp and controls my head. He pulls my head to his cock. I open my mouth and take him inside. Adam fucks my face hard, just to the edge of what I can handle without gagging.

Suddenly, he pulls my head off his cock. He gives me a condom. I am more than proficient with this now. He spins me around and pulls my hips downward so I am sitting on his cock. "Look at him. Look at him while I fuck you." He yanks my head up so my eyes meet the sub's. Adam fucks me rather brutally, smacking my ass, thighs, or breasts each time I drop my head. Again and again my eyes connect with the subs, who passively sits, watching this scene unfold. At one point, Adam pulls my hair till my chin is high in the air. I put my hand on my clit and begin to massage it in deep circles. Adam yanks my arm and replaces my hand with his. He presses against my pubic bone, moving his hand back and forth. I lose myself in the rhythm of his thrusts and the motion of his hand. We cum together, Adam thrusting hard into me and holding himself there so I feel the pulsing of his cock as he cums. The sub watches attentively.

Adam lifts me up and turns me around to face him. "Clean me up" is all he says. I kneel down and remove the condom and then lick his softening penis clean. I look up to see if this meets his approval. He smiles. Adam, leans to the right, looking at the sub, "You may go." The sub lowers his eyes and leaves quietly, demurely now. I wonder what is next.

Adam grabs my sides with more tenderness now and lifts me up. He sits me on his lap facing him and begins to kiss my neck, ears, cheeks, and forehead rather tenderly. I feel relief and joy. I realize how much I want, no, need his affection. We make out passionately, our hands stroking and caressing the other. In short order, Adam's cock awakens. I attempt to move down so I can suck on it, but Adam holds me in place. He asks me, "Catherine, should we make love?" I don't know what to say. This whole time I have simply been told what to do and faced a consequence when I didn't comply quickly enough. He senses my uncertainty and asks, "Catherine, I would like to make love with you. Is that all right?" Wow. My mind is blown. I don't answer with words. Instead, I reach for another condom, letting our eyes meet, I smile.

He carries me to the bed, laying me down like a precious doll. He lies beside me, stroking my hair, and whispering my name into my ear. I am over the moon. I roll on top of him and he doesn't resist. I slide his now fully erect penis into my cunt, dripping wet from the prolonged foreplay. I fuck him the way I want to and he lets me. When I am close to cumming, I press down hard against him and tilt my pelvis so my clit is pressed hard against his public bone. My legs quiver and I am unable to move for a moment. Adam gently grabs my hips and keeps the motion and thus my orgasm going.

I slide one leg down straight, lay on his chest hugging him, and then roll us both so now he is on top. I pull my knees up, locking my ankles together. Each time I cum in this position, I pull him hard against me with the circle of my legs and then squeeze my thighs so that my clit is pressed against him and any thrusts he makes increases the intensity of my orgasm. I am awash with pleasure, lost in the moment, and completely in bliss. I realize I am tuned into myself only and it's a lovely thing. I am focused on what gives me the most pleasure and Adam is going along with all of it. I find my voice, "Adam, will you fuck me from behind? Will you allow yourself to cum when I do?"

"Yes, sweet Catherine, I will."

Today, we clean up and relax together. The pace feels leisurely. We refill the tub with warm water several times. We towel each other off and Adam carries me to a daybed where he massages body lotion all over me. He pauses and pulls my feet up and then spreads my knees apart, his entire focus on my crotch. He gently strokes the labia and uses two fingers to spread them apart, revealing my vagina. "You are a thing of beauty, Catherine. I love how you taste and smell. I love how wet you get when we make love. And I miss you." My heart leaps in my chest. I am totally taken aback.

He continues, "It's all right for us to feel things for the other. Our connection is very deep, and how could it be otherwise? And we need to slowly, gently back away from this because however sweet this is, and it is sweet indeed, it is not about attachment. It is about you and you alone. I am here to serve you and meet your needs, even those needs you are unaware of."

I feel a pain in my chest and my eyes well up with tears. He sees this and smiles sweetly, pulling me close and saying my name over and over. My tears flow with quiet but persistent sobs. He just holds me, rocking me like a child, saying my name.

I arrive home exhausted and distraught. Of course, S has anticipated this and a basket awaits me. My assistant instantly can tell things are amiss. The ever-cool Catherine is clearly not herself. My assistant doesn't even ask what I want. Instead, she hurries off and returns shortly with a tray of small bites, a bowl of tomato basil soup, a large pot of cardamom ginger tea, and even a shot glass and a bottle of fine brandy. She tells me to ring the bell when I want supper.

I settle into my most comfortable chair and wrap a cashmere throw around my shoulders, pouring myself a cup of tea and a shot of brandy, I open S's note.

Dearest Catherine,

You are at a key juncture in your journey. You are moving out onto your own. It can feel like jumping off a cliff, this letting go of the old, even letting go of the very recent. As humans, we cling to things, people, relationships out of some need to make permanent what is impermanent. True liberation lies in not trying to capture and freeze the moment but to flow through it. However, it takes experience to know this and you are on the edge of that experience. Until then, trust. Trust that everything is focused on you, what you need and what will support your journey. Remember the dichotomy: pain and pleasure are two sides of the same coin. Once you truly know that, you realize it is you who decides what is pleasure and what is pain. There is beauty in everything. It is us who limit it by drawing distinctions. See the beauty in how you feel right now. See the beauty in your longing, your fear, your brokenness.

- *S*

I hear myself sigh. God, that woman is good. Dang. Her words are unbelievably comforting. I take a sip of the fragrant tea and realize how delicious it is, how soothing, how perfect it is. I cast my eyes toward the tray of bites. Yum. What should I nibble first?

Before I go to sleep, I add to my list of things I am learning:

- I am learning to love myself
- I am learning to be vulnerable and open with others
- I understand, though haven't fully internalized (yet), that permanence is an illusion

- The place to live is in the flow. The flow is life.
- The trappings of what humans refer to as life - possessions, money, children, prestige - are indeed "traps". We focus on collecting these instead of being in and living the moment.
- I think I can fall in love and I want to.

S invites me to meet with her. She shares that she is including someone else in the meeting, assuring me this will be perfect. Hmmm. What does she have planned now?

The meeting is not at the House of S. Instead, we are meeting for dinner and drinks at a quiet but well-established restaurant. I wonder, who else in this restaurant knows S and in what capacity do they know her? S had assured me that confidentiality and privacy are top-of-mind. I decide to go along. S has been exactly who she says she is up until now. I trust her.

We are meeting on a Wednesday. I stay at work to wrap up a few details on some due-diligence for a potential IPO. I am wearing a classic shift dress in teal wool with a jacket from my favorite British clothing line, The Fold. (I love wearing clothes not readily available in the US. It's part of my persona to stand out, however subtly.) The sub collar sits on my neck. I've matched the polished stainless steel with a statement piece from a boutique designer from India.

My driver arrives 20 minutes before the meeting time. I settle into the back and reflexively touch the collar. Odd how it grounds me, makes me feel safe. We pull up to the restaurant on time, and with a deep breath, I step out of the car. It feels very much like the first time I stepped into the House of S -- new, unknown territory ahead.

The maitre 'd is expecting me and ushers me to a corner table. S is dressed in an elegant but understated Chanel suit. It looks like a piece from the 1980's. S has a remarkably flat stomach and the cream-colored pencil skirt is draped on her hips with a classic Karl Lagerfeld's chain and fabric belt. The jacket is a wool knit, cream-colored with black piping accents on shelves, pockets, and collar. She presents herself so elegantly with such grace and confidence, I find myself wishing I were more like her.

A striking man, Masao Tashiki, is the other guest. Where to begin describing him? Hmmm. There is a smokiness about this man, like a charcoal drawing where someone has taken a gum eraser and softened the edges. He is immaculately groomed and his clothes, while understated, are clearly expensive. Like me, he is wearing business attire -- a custom-tailored suit that reveals a muscular body. I suspect he is a few years younger than I am but it's hard to tell. He reaches out his hand to shake mine and our eyes meet for the first time. "I'm Masao. My friends call me Mas. Please, Catherine, -- it's Catherine, isn't it? Please, feel free to call me Mas."

It's like the cheesiest moment ever, I mean, like a movie where the two main characters meet and there's a cut-away to cartoon fireworks. Holy fuck. I feel my lower lip quiver. Me, Catherine Standish Bolton, brought to her proverbial knees. I swallow and recover at least some of my composure, extending my hand. When we shake hands, he delays releasing mine ever so slightly, and when I look up, there is a twinkle in his eyes. The game is on.

S has taken the liberty of ordering a series of small plates -- olives cured with lemon peel, garlic, olive oil, and salt; a fusion twist on caviar blini -- finely chopped hard-boiled egg, green onion, caviar, and sour cream over a very thin layer of rice, rolled in seaweed and presented like sushi; polenta with the freshest tomato sauce, drizzled with basil oil and topped with Parmigiano Reggiano...The plates come and go as S and I drink a crisp prosecco and Mas sips chilled Absolut Elyx.

I learn that Mas is also in finance but on the west coast. He is opening a new headquarters for his company, Technology Systems (TS), on the east coast. After a string of successful IPOs for tech start-ups, TS is a rising star in the financial world. Representation on both coasts is essential going forward. Mas will head up the east coast office and continue as CFO for TS.

I watch him talk. He is measured and articulate, but there is a way that he pauses and looks directly into my eyes that I suspect is not how he speaks to everyone. I find myself wondering what, if anything, he knows about me. I get my answer quickly.

"Catherine, I've followed your career for a long time. You've done a remarkable job of keeping Bolton FInancial on a growth path with very few, if any, bumps in the road. Quite impressive, I must say. And the recent write up of your masterful handling of the Coach and Company merger with Crump and Sons in the Wall Street Journal, God, I could only wish for that kind of press for TS."

Normally, I would respond by saying thank you, the credit for success should go to my staff, etc. Instead, I take things in a new direction entirely: "It's really flattering that you read that article. That merger was one of the trickier deals of late. Mas, I wonder if you are as curious as I am about tonight's introduction." I pause and turn my head toward S. "S, I am sure you have a motive for bringing us both here. I have to say, that's really what's top-of-mind for me." I stop there, punctuating my last sentence with a short breath in and out, dropping my shoulders and keeping my gaze on S, who seems as immovable as ever.

S smiles, lifting her chin up. "Catherine, I wondered how long it would be before we addressed this. You are not one for dancing around the edges." S now focuses on Mas. "Before I say more, I need both of you," -- S looks at each of us in turn -- "to review some confidentiality agreements. Each of you has already signed a blanket agreement, but these are specific to the two of you."

Both Mas and I simultaneously sit up a bit, straightening our backs, taking in a breath. Okay then, this is a House of S connection. My, my, how titillating.

S pushes paper in each of our directions. The document is short and to the point. *Any activity, connection, sexual interaction that occurs at the location known as the House of S between said parties is to remain confidential. Any breach of confidentiality, including but not limited to, private or public conversations, emails, letters, press releases are subject to damages between the parties in the sum of $1,000,000 or higher as awarded by the court. Each party will deposit a sum of $500,000 in an escrow account maintained at Barclays Bank. Such deposit will be forfeited and shared equally between the House of S and the aggrieved party upon proof provided to the House of S that such confidentiality has been violated. This is in addition to the court award.*

Okey dokey. S isn't kidding around. As always, she has thought of all the details. After all, Mas (apparently) and I are both clients of S, and yet the nature of our work makes such a connection very tricky. S shares that there won't be any further information revealed until the escrow amounts are deposited and the additional confidentiality agreement is signed, notarized, and returned. Fair enough. It's the price...literally...to be paid for notoriety. The evening ends with more questions swirling in my head. Clearly, S has a plan (as always) and it involved Mas and me.

A weekend goes by with no trip to the House of S. It's the first such weekend in months, and I fill the void with catching up at work and laying the groundwork for an expansion in small-private offerings, a lucrative but time intensive area of finance. Sunday evening I receive this note:

Catherine,

Thank you for both your patience and discretion. You and Mas have completed all the steps to begin. I would like to meet next with each of you to explain upcoming opportunities. I feel this will be an important next step in your journey. Let's aim for a mid-week meeting, all right?

S

Wednesday finds me at the House of S around 6 pm. An assistant ushers me into S's office and points to the chair facing S's desk. I guess the intimate seating area next to the window doesn't suit the nature of the conversation she has planned.

Instead of the usual wine or drink, I am offered coffee, tea, or sparkling water. I choose the latter and take a breath. It feels like a shift is in the air and the anticipation is killing me.

S walks in and apologizes for being delayed. "Catherine, I can imagine you very much want to know what's afoot, yes? And I also know you understand and support the need for an additional enforcement of confidentiality. You and Mas operate in the same sphere. It's important to preserve your security. Luckily, you both were prompt and all is sorted, so let's talk about what's ahead."

I hear my response in my head! "Yes, let's!"

"So Catherine, I feel you are ready to take on an equal, someone who might even become an important person in your life. How important, of course, is up to you and Mas, but I felt the energy between you two last week and can imagine this will only grow."

S pauses and then clears her throat, a signal that the punchline is at hand: "I am proposing several sessions -- at least two -- where each of you takes turns calling the shots. Mas will be the designer of a scene and you the participant. Then the following week, you will design a scene and Mas will be the participant. You each may choose the role(s) you wish to explore. I will operate as a resource in your planning, and, of course, as the point person to assure all resources - human and otherwise - are in place. The initial commitment from each of you is just the first two sessions."

She pauses again to allow this all to sink in. I hear my in-breath and feel my eyes widen. Wow. "S, I am intrigued, of course. Why the shift? I mean, I was learning a lot through my interaction with Adam." I find myself reflexively touching the collar Adam gave me that I am wearing under my shirt.

"There is no doubt, Catherine, no doubt at all. And you were also becoming quite close to Adam, weren't you?"

I feel the color rise a bit in my cheeks. Close? Yeah, we were becoming close…

"Catherine, I am just suggesting that it's time for you to step out and meet someone on a more equal footing. This will be an important transition from a learning posture to a maintaining posture. And let me define maintaining. What I mean is, at some point, you will both want and need to create your own scenes, whether for pleasure or simply to spice things up. Pleasure and spice are necessary elements of sustainable connections. And I do believe you are ready for something sustainable."

Something sustainable. In the personal realm, I have no idea what that means. I have barely dated in the last two decades. Every moment until recently has been devoted to building Bolton Financial. And then there is the question of whether I can ever sustain a relationship.

S, apparently a mind-reader, continues, "Catherine, you have changed in the last few months. Long term connections -- relationships -- take some discipline. You are a very disciplined person. I believe you can, indeed, sustain meaningful connections. I think you haven't had the time or space to do so until recently. Like anything else, connections take discipline and work as well as coaching. Experience can be a teacher, though sometimes a painful one. The journey you have been actively working through with Adam has helped you develop greater range in the expression of who you are. It has opened up possibilities you didn't even know existed. Now, it's time to put that learning into practice with someone who doesn't yet know you well."

S sat back, satisfied with her explanation. She cocked her head slightly and waited. I swear my exhale was audible down the hall. It was a long, slow outbreathing that was more than just pushing carbon dioxide out in order to pull more oxygen in. It was the sound of resigned commitment to step out into new territory.

I had never worried about finding a partner. My busy and successful life has been incredibly satisfying, though clearly it has consumed me. I had no problem finding casual sexual partners. Some I even sustained for long stretches of time. But, a relationship? No. Not even close. Relationships seemed messy, complicated, distracting. As long as my basic need for sex and physical intimacy was met, I was good. I had no need or energy for more, or so I thought.

Then came Adam, and the most unexpected things happened. I had no idea one could build remarkable connectedness through intense physical intimacy, that that intimacy could proceed and then create that remarkable connectedness.

What's even more surprising is that I even wanted this. And yet, when I think of Adam, I feel both a deep longing and a sense of peace and beauty. It is an odd feeling, neither sad nor happy. The peace and beauty come from the connection. The longing comes from a realization that the connection is fragile. I have no confidence in my ability to sustain a relationship over time. This is new territory for me, and however attracted I am to Mas, I am also terrified I will mess things up. And, for the first time in my life, I am willing to try.

"All right. I am excited and not just a wee bit anxious, but I am game."

"Perfect place to be, Catherine. Then it's set. We will start this Saturday."

I do my best to focus for the remainder of the week. I am only partially successful, but my team pulls through and I appreciate how competent and thorough they are.

Saturday arrives and I am up early. Like a schoolgirl before her first dance, I fret about how I look, and in the end, I decide on minimum makeup, focusing instead on careful placement of ylang ylang, jasmine, and rose essential oils behind my ears, back of the neck, wrists, cleavage, top of my thighs, and ankles. I don't worry about my clothes, as I know these won't be what I wear, and then I start wondering, what will I wear?

Soon enough, I have the answer, and it's not what I was expecting. There is no wardrobe change, no halter, no collar, no teddy, no thong, no kimono. I am to wear what I came in. Shit. Fuck. Damn. I wish I had somehow anticipated this. Oh well, mom jeans, a white t-shirt, and Birkenstocks will have to do. Fuck. I am not offered champagne or alcohol, just sparkling water. I feel a bit desperate for something to relax me and calm my nerves, but, no, not on offer today it seems. Strange.

My assistant greets me warmly and takes me straight away to the top floor. She ushers me into a small softly lit room about the size of a large walk-in closet. There are two wooden chairs facing each other. She tells me to have a seat and that Mas will be here soon. I sure hope so. The anticipation is killing me.

A few minutes later, the door opens and Mas steps in. He is dressed casually (thank God) in khakis and a tan t-shirt and hiking sandals, maybe Chacos or Keens. He smiles. I naturally stand up and extend my hair. He smiles again, but doesn't take it.

"Catherine, I imagine we both feel a bit nervous, anxious even. At least, I know I do. I thought we might begin with an exercise that will help us break down our guard a bit, have us see each other as humans, not sex objects or trophies to be snagged. I am doing this largely for myself and I appreciate it if you will go along."

Of course, I am going to go along. That's how this is done, right? "Yes, of course, however you would like." Mas sits in the chair facing me. He pulls it a little closer so we are now almost knee to knee.

"We are going to simply look at each other for 10 minutes. We may blink, of course, but we are to not avert our eyes. It will be hard to do this for the first 3 minutes or so, but it will get easier. Oh, and we won't talk. Not a word for 10 minutes. Understood?" Mas's voice is soothing, not the least bit dominating. It's more level. Even how he said, "Understood?" was different from Adam. Different, but not necessarily bad.

"Yes, I understand. I'll do my best."

He sets a timer on the small table next to his chair. He gives me one more look that invites a response. I smile and say, "Ready when you are," and with that, he clicks start and looks straight into eyes.

Wow. I immediately feel the desire to look away, but I don't. I look back. And I look back. And I look back. It is like looking into a deep well where only as my eyes adjusted to the darkness can I see any detail. It is unnerving but also amazing.

It feels mechanical at first, but as the minutes tick away, I feel my face relax a bit. My vision changes, too. What was sharp and in focus on the periphery, begins to blur and fade away. All I see are his beautiful dark brown eyes looking back. It feels a bit like a fun house room of mirrors with an infinite number of images, each progressively smaller, receding into infinity.

I take a deep breath. He matches it. I swallow. So does he. Yet, no matter what, we keep looking at each other's eyes. I fight the urge to move closer, but it's hard. I am drawn to him.

The timer beeps and I am startled. Mas reaches over and shuts it off. He says, "Catherine, would you come closer. Would you sit on my lap?"

I stand and straddle his legs, gently lowering myself onto his lap. He puts his hands on my lower back. I put mine behind his neck. We are again looking into each other's eyes. He breaks the silence, "Catherine, you are beautiful, and I don't mean just your physical body, which is, indeed, gorgeous, I mean YOU, YOU are beautiful." I feel color rising in my cheeks. I am sixteen again and Mas is my first crush. How many years have passed between then and now? Too many. Way too many.

I feel shy and drop my chin, averting my gaze. Mas brings his right hand up to my chin and gently lifts my head till once again our eyes are locked. "Catherine, I mean it. YOU, the YOU that lives deep inside you, is perhaps the most beautiful thing I have ever seen. May I kiss you?"

My cynical brain wonders when, if ever, the words, "May I..?" ever been uttered in the House of S.

I hear myself saying, "Yes." And with that, our lips touch. I find myself eagerly sucking in his lower lip and nibbling ever so gently on it. His hands are pulling me closer, my hips directly over his crotch. I feel his erection. It is strong and warm. I move my hips against it, a small moan leaves my throat. I push away, wanting to unzip his pants and feel his cock in my mouth, but he stops me.

"Catherine, there is time. Let's savor the moment. I am so happy, I just want to learn how your mouth wants to be worshiped." Oh. My. God. I am fucking melting. We passionately kiss, minutes go by, and my cunt is progressively getting wetter and wetter. I want him to see what he has done. I unzip my jeans, take his hand, and push it down. "See what you have done. I am so wet for you. My cunt aches for you." I am shocked at my language, but it's exactly how I feel. He smiles and begins exploring. Suddenly, he stands me up, takes me by the hand, and walks me to the end of the room where there is a door. Mas opens it. I inhale sharply. Here is a replica of the cabin bedroom and bath. I am stunned.

"S. said you might like this." Mas takes me to the bed. He slowly undresses me, pausing to caress and look. He keeps saying, "You are so beautiful." He attaches cuffs to my wrists and ankles and helps me onto the bed. He clips the cuffs to tethers off each of the four posts. "Catherine, I am doing this so you will be forced to let me go slowly. I want to savor each moment. There is no need for a safe word. I will not hurt you, not now, not ever."

Mas removes his shirt and sandals but keeps his khakis on. He begins at my ankles and feet, tenderly kissing and caressing them. It's nearly unbearable. I am so ready for him to fuck me. But he moves at his pace, seemingly more disciplined than I am. He traces his fingers from my ankles to my cunt and back down the other side. He does this repeatedly, and it is making me crazy. I feel cunt juice leaking out. He must notice this and plants his face between my legs. Oh my God. I push against his mouth. He will not be rushed. He slowly licks from the perineum upwards to my clit. His tongue is firm and the motions persistent and rhythmical. The more he does this, the wetter I become. He raises his head and runs his tongue around his own lips, cleaning off the pearl-colored liquid. He dives back down and furiously attacks my clitoris. I arch my back convulsively and cum hard, squirting. He laps his tongue to catch as much as possible. I am surprised and at first even a bit embarrassed. He looks up, "Oh my God, Catherine, you are a goddess."

He stands up and unclips me. He lets me unbutton his pants. I run my hands underneath the elastic of his briefs teasingly. I see his erection pushing even harder against the fabric. I liberate his cock and begin by just licking the tip where a delicious drop of fluid is hanging. I look up at him and then go all in. I am taking him in my mouth as far back as I can, pulling and pushing on his hips. I feel I am in complete control and it's his turn to submit. I slide his pants down, and using my hands, push his legs apart. This allows me to run the back of my hand from his sacrum over his anus and taint, to the underside of his balls. Each time I do this, I swear his erection grows.

I push him onto the bed on his back. He smiles. I continue licking and sucking until he pulls me on top. He hands me a condom, and I now, with some expertise, put it on him. He lifts my hips up and sets me down on his cock. It is a sublime moment, and I cannot help but cum again. He is holding my hips and lifting me up and down. I am so wet, squishy sounds are audible. He moans and rolls me over.

He pauses to look me in the eyes, "Catherine, I cannot control myself. I am going to cum soon. I promise it won't always be this fast, but I want to lose myself in you. May I?" Again, how strange it feels to be asked for permission in the House of S. I nod my head furiously. I so want to feel him unable to control himself. I want to feel like I am so delectable, he can't delay his hunger.

Mas pauses to suck my breasts and kiss me. Then he inserts his cock with a powerful thrust and I am overcome again. He continues sliding in and out, at times with fury, then clearly pausing to delay the inevitable. But the inevitable finally comes, and I feel his cock pulsing inside me. He is moaning and gasping. He says my name, "Catherine, oh my God, Catherine, you are so beautiful." My legs shiver and quake as I cum again, the full weight of his body lying on mine. We stay in this position, our breathing slowly synchronizing.

Eventually, Mas rolls over and removes the condom. "Catherine, I imagined this moment every day for the last week: how it would be to make love to you, how I would feel. Still, my projections didn't come close to the experience. I am nearly without words. Are you okay if we just lie here a while? I feel I need to just savor this moment a bit."

I nod, close my eyes, and snuggle in next to him. I think at some point we both fall asleep in each other's arms. It's incredible. I just met this man, and yet, I feel so open and hopeful. I feel joyous and scared. I feel like a goddess and like a child.

We wake and Mas smiles at me sweetly. "Let me bathe you, Catherine. I want to worship your body with your permission." I smile and nod. I feel adored and cherished. It is powerful beyond words.

Just like the cabin, there is a large claw-foot tub, big enough for two. Mas begins filling it and adds bubble bath. Oh, yes. I know that scent. Lavender. My God, S., I guess the devil is in the details and you haven't forgotten a single one.

I go to pee and decide at the last moment to leave the door open. Mas notices and he parks himself against the door, leaning against it with the most sweet look. His look is sensual and welcoming. As the stream of urine finally begins to flow, I have a pee-gasm, the pressure of the warm liquid pressing against my still swollen clit. He is pleased. Unexpectedly, he steps in, reaches his hand between my legs and bushes upward to catch a few remaining drops. He brings his hand to his mouth and tastes my piss. "Delicious, Catherine, but you need to drink more water. I think you are dehydrated, my goddess. It's a bit salty."

He takes my hand and leads me to the tub where he helps me slide into the water. He slides in behind me. We rest here for a while as the tub fills, my head resting on his chest, his arms encircling me. I can hear his heart beating. I swear mine is beating the same rhythm. It is magical and intimate and we just met.

Mas takes a sponge and the L'Occitane bar or hand-milled soap. He washes my body likes it's the most precious thing in his world. He slides the soapy sponge over my arms in long strokes. He washes my upper back. He helps me to stand and proceeds to wash my lower back and butt, sliding his hand and sponge between my cheeks and down my legs. He has me turn and face him, still standing. He stands up carefully and then washes the front of my body, my breasts, my crotch, as if it is both a separate delicate gift as well as an extension of himself. He helps me to sit in the tub, now facing him. He takes one of my feet and washes it, carefully attending to the space between each toe. He lets his hand stray down my leg till it reaches my upper thigh. I am in a space that is timeless. I feel like I am in ecstasy with no beginning or end. It is beyond sensual or sexual. It is a celebration of my body as adored by him.

Tears begin to flow. I could not imagine this moment. I could not anticipate my feelings or desire. Yet, here I am, in the presence of this man. I am without words.

Mas honors my feelings and simply continues loving me, continuing to wash my feet and legs. My tears are a slow rain, freely flowing. When he finishes, he gently turns me around and pulls me against his chest again. I rest there, listening to the warm water trickling in with Mas's heartbeat as the bass to this sensual song.

Mas wakes me. I had no idea I had fallen asleep. "Catherine, would you come home with me? I would like to sleep with you tonight." Wow, I think. What a first date. Shit.

And I hear myself say, "Yes, Mas, I would like that." He helps me out of the tub and we dry each other off with the same fluffy towels from the cabin. He lets me dress myself but Mas comes over to brush my hair. He sits me down on the edge of the bed and brushes it with long, gentle strokes. It is loving. It is nurturing.

We leave the House of S in one car. I send my driver home and snuggle into the back seat of Mas's BMW, resting my head against his shoulder. His apartment is downtown. It's sleek and modern with leather and chrome furnishings punctuated by eclectic art pieces.

He's assistant greets us with a slight smile of surprise. He is clearly very discreet but a bit surprised by my unplanned visit.

"Jason, Ms. Bolton will be my guest tonight. Please make sure chef knows. And tomorrow, I don't want anyone disturbing Ms. Bolton or me before 11. We've been working very hard on a project and I imagine we will be up late working on it tonight as well." Mas squeezes my hand slightly. So we have an alibi. I like it.

"Ms. Bolton, what may I get you to drink? I have a lovely Cockburn 1994 Port. It pairs so well with cheese. Might that hit the spot. Oh, and Ms. Bolton, may I call you Catherine, now that we aren't in the office?"

"Yes, of course. What should I call you, Mr. Tashiki?"

"Mas, call me Mas. My first name is Masao, but please call me Mas."

I love our little attempt at sneakiness. It makes our new connection seem even more electric. Mas takes me to a comfortable room off the front hall. Clearly, not his formal entertaining space. This must be where he relaxes. There are shelves with books and keepsakes, a fireplace with a sleek stainless-steel mantel, leather couch flanked by chrome and leather chairs with mid-century floor lamps.

Mas tells me to get comfortable and that there is a powder room beyond the door to the right. He wants to make sure all is well in the kitchen.

I settle into one of the chairs. They are unbelievably comfortable. A few minutes later, Mas returns. He is carrying a vase full of flowers -- jasmine, tuberose, roses, vining honeysuckle. "S picked these out. She said the scent would suit you." God, she knows me well. Smell is everything.

"They are beautiful. You are so thoughtful. I am really touched." I stand and go to smell the arrangement, making sure the back of my hand brushes against his. Our eyes meet and I feel warmth between my legs. God, I like this man.

The chef comes in with a large tray and places it on the glass coffee table. There is a gorgeous array of cheeses - Bleu, Emmental, Camembert, and yes, Schloss cheese from California, the Rouge et Noir Company, to be exact. How thoughtful of S. to share this gustatory secret. Swirls of pear slices, clusters of red grapes, guava paste, and at least three types of crackers fill the tray. Mas brings over the port and two glasses. The pale ruby color is matched by a divine fragrance. Mas raises his glass and proposes a toast, "To us, and wherever that journey takes us."

To us…

The night is both magical and surreal. Mas insists we not have sex, but would simply enjoy being in each other's presence. Clearly, he has much more discipline than I do. We nibble on cheese and sip port, enjoy a light dinner, and then, when the staff retires for the evening, head upstairs to his bedroom. (Mas insists that we mess up the bed in the guest room and make it look like I stayed there. I am wondering what we will do in the future. I am surprised I am thinking there IS a future.)

Mas looks into my eyes and asks if he could help me undress. The words feel sexy, like I am about to lose my virginity oh so gently and deliciously. He pulls my t-shirt over my head and stops. We are inches apart facing each other. He is taller but not by so much, maybe five inches. Mas puts his hands on my shoulders and pushes me back slightly so we can better look into each other's eyes. "Catherine, I could look into your eyes for days." I smile shyly and drop my chin and lower my eyes. He takes his right hand and gently raises my chin again. "I mean it, Catherine. You are so complex and interesting. There is so much to you I want to know and understand. I hope you feel the same way."

How do I feel? Good question. These words pop into my head: excited, hopeful, scared, determined, anxious, and happy. Is there a feeling word that encompasses "all over the map"? Because that is where I am. All over the map.

Mas traces his fingers along the outline of my arms down to my hands. He gathers my fingers in his and brings our arms to the center in a sort of two-person namaste pose while he keeps looking into my eyes. "Catherine, I want to tell you about why I began going to the House of S. I want you to know my story. I think it's important that we each understand the other's history, how we got to this moment." I nod. "I'd like to share this with you when I am holding your naked body in my arms. I think it will be easier for me to be honest and open if our clothes are removed. It's kind of like our armor, right? I want us to take the armor off." I'd never quite thought of it this way, but it certainly was true, especially for people in finance where the wrong suit, tie, or color communicated weakness and the right ones quite the opposite.

He begins to unbutton his shirt. I touch his hands, and he lets me take on this task. I feel his skin on the back of my fingers. I close my eyes for a moment, wanting to take a sensory snapshot of this moment. I slide the shirt off his shoulders and fold it casually, setting it down on a nearby chair. Mas unzips my jeans and slowly works them down off my hips. I have an easier time with his khakis as his hips are straighter. We are now facing each other in our underwear. He reaches around my back and unclasps my bra, pulling the shoulder straps gently forward. He lets the bra drop to the ground, keeping his eyes on mine. He uses the back of his hands to gently explore the curves of my breasts. I take a deep breath in and close my eyes. Sensory snapshot number 2.

I step closer and slip my hands under the elastic waist of his boxers, moving my hands to the back as I slide them down, letting my hands cup his cheeks briefly. Mas's eyes are closed. Is he taking a sensory snapshot?

Mas's cock is not erect or flaccid. It's in a luscious, tempting in-between state. But I leave it be, however much I want to touch or suck on it. He opens his eyes and smiles. When he slides my underwear down, he goes down on his knees, face at my crotch. He kisses the triangular area above my clit, above the small landing strip of pubic hair I maintain. He stands back up, takes my hand, and leads me to the bed, peeling back the covers, he helps me in before sliding in on the other side. He cuddles up and simply holds me for minutes or hours. I have no sense of time.

He then begins sharing his story, unfolding parts of his life in the same gentle way he undressed me. "I come from a rather typical first-generation immigrant family. My parents held down numerous jobs, many well below their actual qualifications. My dad was a fully qualified accountant and my mother, a teacher, but their immigrant status prevented them from ever holding those positions in their new country. They really poured themselves into their children, my sister, Keika, and me."

"The pressure to excel was huge. Their intentions were the best, but there was a cost. Keika was particularly gifted with the oboe. She plays with the San Francisco Symphony. Luckily, because she is female, my parents' rather relentless pressure was less. She was allowed to date. My parents felt they had done the needful when Keika married a lawyer. Rather predictable, eh? Marrying your daughter off successfully?"

"My story was equally predictable. I put all my focus into studying. I managed to get into several Ivy League schools and my parents chose Cal Berkeley instead, followed by Stanford Business School. My parents felt the need to keep me close by so I wouldn't be tempted to stray from the plan."

"While the plan included eventual marriage and children, it didn't include happiness or fulfilment per se. It certainly didn't include marrying anyone outside of a narrow band of what my parents deemed appropriate. I don't resent them for this. I understand their motivations. They truly were doing what they thought best. Still, there was a cost."

"My response to their pressure was to double down on work. I did have a string of hook-ups. In fact, that's all I have had. I have no real experience with connecting in a meaningful, intimate way with another. I was adept at the physical act but rather clueless about true intimacy, so I avoided it."

"My parents grew increasingly disappointed. I completed all the tick marks regarding career and none of those dealing with family. I repeatedly promised to get married and have kids and then turned around and ignored any women they referred to me. My sister rose in their estimation and I remained the prodigal son. Then my dad was diagnosed with cancer. I was both relieved and guilty. Guilty that I had yet to complete their plan. Relieved that at least some of the pressure would ebb when he died. Crazy, huh? Crazy to actually think the death of a parent could be a relief."

At this point, Mas stops talking. He holds me a bit closer. I can feel his respiration rate increase. And then, a tear falls on my shoulder. And then another one. And another one. He doesn't sob. He just cries quietly.

I am not certain how to respond, so I just let him hold me and cry. I feel his vulnerability. Before, I would have seen this as a weakness. Now, I see it as a strength. Mas is willing to face the difficult, the uncomfortable, and be open and truthful. That is a strength. Am I at the point of being able to do this?

I guess we fall asleep. I wake up with morning light shining through the half-open blinds. We have somehow exchanged positions. I have rolled over and am spooning him. He stirs, turns over, and looks into my eyes. "Catherine, you are so beautiful. I know I said we shouldn't make love, but that was for last night. Might I make love to you this morning?"

I nod and smile. "Catherine, don't pee yet. I want your bladder to be full. Your orgasm will be stronger." Mas throws back the duvet and rolls me onto my back. He smiles as he goes down between my legs. I am gripping the bottom sheet with my hands as Mas keeps bringing me to the edge and then pulling back. It is at once delightful and excruciating. Finally, he lets me cum and I cum hard, body shaking, back arching, and a gush of liquid squirting from my cunt. He lifts his head, cunt juice covering his lips and chin. "There's a good girl. So, good." He slides up next to me and begins kissing me. "I want you to know how you taste."

I feel his cock, hard and erect pressing against my hip. Mas rolls me onto my left hip and slides into my cunt from behind. He brings his right hand around to stimulate my clit. He begins making larger movements, passing over my clit in increasingly small circles. He matches the movement of his hips to the movement of his hand, and I cum again and again. He begins to increase his tempo, pressing his cock deeper and against my g-spot. My full bladder makes everything tighter. He whispers, "I am going to cum. Cum with me, babe." With that, I let go. My heads falls back.

"Oh my God, Mas. I am cumming. I am cumming. Please, don't stop, Mas." He deftly obliges, even as he cums, he keeps sliding in and out, pressing against my g-spot. He is moaning and gripping me tightly. I feel his body shudder and my legs are shaking. We are a harmonious mess of bodily fluid, sweat, and rapture.

I meet with S. on Tuesday to review the plan for the following Saturday. She is curious what my goals are, what I hope to accomplish. We are again sitting face to face in the two overstuffed chairs near the window, sipping champagne and eating petit eclairs.

"S., I want to know if Mas can take full control of me. I want to know if I can feel completely at his mercy and still trust him. I need to know this. It's a test of sorts. Can I trust him even when I am at my most vulnerable?"

"Catherine, I think your plan will accomplish that, but I think you'll need to give Mas a heads-up. I suggest a note, so he understands how what he will do will serve you."

After a final review, I leave to head home to draft a note. I will run it by S. before sending it on to Mas.

Mas, I am planning our session for this Saturday, and I need to give you some background. I know I haven't yet shared my story. I fully intend to, but it may take me some time. One thing you need to know is that for me to trust you, I need to experience what it is like to be at your mercy. I need to be helpless and I need you to be rough with me.

I know you said you would never hurt me. How I will know that is, paradoxically, if you hurt me a little, not from anger but from arousal, with the goal of heightening tension and pleasure. S. has agreed to work with you before Saturday so you are comfortable with this.

I know you said we don't need a safe word. In this case, you will need to be attune to me. You'll need to discern when too much is too much. And in this regard, I will be completely vulnerable. And that is exactly where I need to be to learn to trust you.

Catherine

S. approves my note and I send it off to Mas with the addition of a few drops of essential oils. I don't know how important smell is to him, but it is one powerful way for me to bond with another. I remind myself to ask him for an article of clothing, one he wears close to his body, so I can sleep with it when we aren't together. I realize in this moment that I haven't thought of Adam for a few days. I consider what this means. Maybe S. was right. Maybe I am ready for something sustainable. I think of Mas -- how his body felt snuggled up to mine, how he allowed himself to cry in my presence, how it felt when we came together in a fury of moans and quakes -- and I feel warmth growing between my legs. I am connecting with him, and it is beautiful.

The week goes by smoothly. My work with my staff prior to the cabin trip continues to pay dividends. They are showing mature and competent judgment. I am thinking there may be opportunities for vacations in my future. Living, not just a life. It might become a reality.

Saturday arrives and I am up early. I have a wardrobe change planned, so I choose yoga pants, t-shirt, and sneakers. I focus on my make-up -- not too much as likely I will be sweating -- but enough to accent my eyes, cheekbones, and lips. I apply my special mix of jasmine, rose, mogra, and sandalwood in all the right places. As I sweat, my scent will fill the room.

I step into the House of S. The familiar heavy doors swing open and welcome me. This time it will be a scene of my design. I cannot know how Mas will do, but I know what is planned.

My assistant meets me with a smile. She has done her homework and selected the most alluring outfit. It's an elaborate red harness that fits perfectly. No thong. No bra. Simply a leather structure to make it easy for him to move my body.

She has something else -- the key to the necklace Adam gave me. I sit down at the vanity table, and nod my ascent, and she unlocks the collar. She replaces the metal collar with a red leather one, one that will come off when today's scene is done. I feel a bit like a graduate. No diploma, no cap and gown. Just a journey to finding myself.

My assistant pulls my hair into a ponytail high on my head. This will make it easier for Mas to control my head, should he choose to. On goes the kimono, and after one last trip to the washroom, she and I are off.

The scene starts with me being clipped into the cross frame once again, my back to the room. My assistant makes the adjustments so the tethers are tight and hold me fast. She leaves after turning on the spotlights. I feel the warmth of the lights on my shoulders and buttocks. I am ready.

I hear the door open and Mas enters. Already, I feel my pulse quicken. He goes to the table and selects an instrument. He steps behind me and says, "Catherine, are you ready?" I nod. He begins.

He has chosen a riding crop. The small surface area makes for a stinging strike. The short length prevents the strikes from being too harsh. He is a bit tentative at first, striking less tender areas like my calves. But his confidence grows, and he begins to strike my buttocks and inner thighs. Sweat builds on my forehead. It is the unknowing that is largely responsible for this. *How long will this last? Where will the next strike land? How much will it hurt?*

Mas is going slowly, pausing, I imagine, to check on my well-being. As my head begins to droop, the tempo slows. He stops and unclips the cuffs from the tethers and turns me around. He reclips me and begins to work the front. It's a shorter session but far more intense. He is focused on my breasts, stomach, and upper thighs. He punctuates his strikes with strikes to my clit. I make audible gasps. While I am not looking at Mas, I feel his eyes on me. He drops the crop and gathers me in his arms, saying, "Oh, Catherine, I hope I have pleased you. I so want to give you what you need."

He unclips me and carries me to the adjacent room and lays me on the bed. He gently removes the harness and collar. He massages arnica into my skin and applies cool packs. He kisses me gently on the forehead, shoulders, hands, and feet.

"Catherine, you are the most intriguing human I've ever met. Ethereal, really. I hope I have served you well today."

I smile and nod. He feeds me sips of water and slides an arnica tab under my tongue. He turns on the bath, the scent of lavender bubble bath fills the room. When it's full, he gathers me in his arms and slides me into the bath. He takes off his clothes and joins me, pulling me back to rest against his chest. We drift off to a temporal dreamland. He whispers, "Come home and stay with me tonight, Catherine. I need to hold you."

I wake up next to Mas. Again, the morning light is coming in through half-closed blinds. He is snuggled behind me with one arm draped over my mid-section. My hand finds its way to his cock. He has a lovely morning erection. I roll over and dive down below the duvet to pay this lovely organ its due. He wakes up and begins to run his hands through my hair. He grabs a handful of hair right next to my scalp and uses this leverage to lay me on my back. He reaches into the nightstand and puts on a condom. He climbs on and rubs his penis up and down my vulva, spreading the seeping liquid till the outside is slippery and wet. He presses in hard and fast, holding my butt cheeks in his hands, bringing my hips to meet his. He fucks me hard, pushing deeply. I feel my breath quicken. He responds and increases his tempo. We climax together, gripping each other hard. He stays on top of me until our breathing quiets and synchronizes. He gently rolls off.

"Catherine, I adore you. Do you feel this?"

I pause, smile, and consider the question. "Mas, I feel so much, especially after yesterday. I feel I owe you a bit of my story, but not in this moment. Will you come to my house tonight? I think I need to be in familiar surroundings to be able to talk about this. Is that all right?"

I immediately feel regret. I don't really like talking about myself and I certainly don't want to derail the unfolding of our connection with my baggage. Mas must sense something is up because he speaks up rather quickly, "Catherine, I very much want to know you, ALL of you. I really want to hear about where you have come from. I think sharing these things -- being open about our wounds -- will show how much we trust each other. We'll have to learn how to be vulnerable human beings. It's especially hard for us coming from such a cut-throat field, but still, we must try if there is to be a future between us."

I sigh. He is right. This is where the rubber hits the road. It's been so easy to simply hook-up with people. Nurturing a relationship? Now that's hard.

I have my cook make sushi. I later rethink my choice. Will Mas feel I am pandering to his background? Oh well, too late now. When Mas arrives, my assistant ushers him into my library. It's the most intimate space in my apartment with ample overstuffed leather chairs, rather dim overall lighting, and walls lined with books and interesting objects.

"Mas, I asked my cook to make sushi. I then completely questioned my judgment. I didn't want you to think I am simply making assumptions about what you like to eat based on the origin of your name. I just really like to eat sushi when friends come over. There's a certain intimacy in just sharing food from a common plate." I stop there and try to read his face. He smiles broadly.

"Oh, Catherine. No need to overthink this. I do love sushi and would likely love it whether or not my heritage was Japanese! Now, the question is, are we drinking warm or cold sake?"

It's lovely evening. We eat at a small writing table in the library, drinking warm sake. I share my journey with a bit more detail than originally intended, likely goaded on by the sake glow. I talk about the hollowness I felt in my success, that somehow the better Bolton Financial did, the less alive I felt. And I shared my experience with Adam. It was cathartic. I found myself talking about that connection in past tense. It was an important part of the journey, but not the destination.

Mas is an incredible listener. Occasionally, he stops me to ask a clarifying question. Other times, he gracefully paraphrases to make sure he understands. I love it when he summarizes by laying out so clearly what I have shared. I feel deeply understood.

This is so much more than I felt with Adam. When I think back, what we had was lots of shared physical interaction. We shared very little of our lives. I don't realize that until I consider how it feels to be opening up to Mas.

When I finish, Mas takes a deep breath and says, "I wasn't really able to tell the whole story the other night about why I ended up at the House of S. I was really feeling emotional about my relationship with my dad and the guilt I felt and feel even today about my dad's diagnosis. If it's all right, I'd like to finish." I reach out and touch his hand, holding his gaze for a moment, and nod.

"My father's illness really consumed all the energy in the family. I was able to use this as cover, to keep the conversation off me and on him. His cancer treatment simply slowed the decline. It became clear he was going to succumb to the disease."

"As my father began to realize this, he really began to press. He wanted me to commit to getting married. It almost didn't matter at that point to whom. I did a very foolish thing. I promised I would marry a woman of their choosing. Within two weeks, we gathered for a civil ceremony, my dad attending in a wheelchair, and I married a woman I barely knew."

"I honestly did my best to suck it up and make it work. I reminded myself how many arranged marriages around the world result ultimately in deep loving relationships. But no matter how much I tried, I felt absolutely nothing for my wife. Even worse, she knew it. One night, I asked her if we could talk. I told her that what I was going to share would be painful but we needed to figure things out. I told her about my parents' pressure and my guilt around not fulfilling their dreams for me. I talked about how I allowed that guilt to say yes to something -- someone -- when I knew in my heart I would struggle. I told her that I did want it to work but that wanting it to work and having it work were two different things."

"When I finished, she sighed and merely thanked me for my honesty. She proposed we divorced once my dad passed away. And that's what we did. The only solace I take away from this humiliating failure is that she is now happily married with kids."

"Sadly, my mother is struggling to forgive me. We don't speak regularly. And honestly, Catherine, my biggest regret is that I have never learned what a meaningful relationship that isn't transactional looks like. I went to the House of S to learn to connect and be vulnerable."

"S is an incredibly insightful human. She saw my vulnerability and my hunger, and she knew just what to do. Unlike your work with Adam, S had me meet with different partners -- women and men -- each week. She used each experience to take me closer and closer to my core until I found that raw place that I had been so desperately avoiding. It was never about my partners. It was clearly all about me. My partners were simply a mirror I could look into and see my reflection, or not. I have come to terms with my choices. I have come to realize I do want to connect, be open and vulnerable, with another person. And Catherine, I would like that person to be you."

I hadn't considered that this moment would come so quickly. I feel a deep attraction to Mas, but I am feeling overwhelmed at the thought of committing. I realize this is not about Mas but only about me. "Mas, I need time. I am just getting to a place where I can love myself. Are you willing to wait for me to get my head straight? Can we keep seeing each other?"

He smiles softly, just the corners rising up. "Of course, Catherine. I realized the moment the words left my mouth, it is too soon."

I reach over again and touch his hand. I wait until a few seconds pass so he can see my eyes and read my face for clues. "Mas, I am incredibly attracted to you. I very much want to see where this goes." I squeeze his hand. He turns his over and takes mine.

"All right then. What are our next steps?"

I smile and we negotiate our schedules. We also agree to debrief separately with S.

Mas and I have our first date planned for Tuesday -- drinks at a rooftop bar and then a quiet dinner at an Italian restaurant known for its amazing gnocchi. We've both come straight from work, so we look like a power couple. I kind of like that. Mas proposes we drink something celebratory. We settle on Bellinis. The air is the perfect temperature and the view, dazzling. Soon, the mood is relaxed, fun, and yes, celebratory. It feels like we are an old couple, two people who've been together more than a handful of times. I take note of this.

Dinner is yummy and intimate. We are seated well away from other diners. Mas somehow manages to stroke my inner thigh under the tablecloth while acting like absolutely nothing is going on. I mouth these words to him: *You are so naughty. You are making me wet.* This simply encourages him.

To my surprise and delight, tiramisu appears with a candle in it. I look to Mas for an explanation, and he smiles at the waiter and says, "It's our two-week anniversary." Ever poised, the waiter smiles back and extends his congratulations. Mas insists on feeding me dessert with his fork. It feels sexy and tender and bonding. Per our plan for the evening, we say good-bye at the restaurant and head to our respective homes. I really want to sleep with him, but I do understand some element of anticipation is a good thing, so I head home.

My meeting with S is a simple debrief. I share my concern about not being ready to commit. She nods. "Catherine, we are the story we tell ourselves. The key is to figure out the story you'd LIKE to tell yourself and then tell yourself THAT story over and over until you believe it." God, I wish it were that simple.

"How do I interrupt the story that I DON'T like that is playing in my head, the one that tells me I will surely mess this up and so why bother trying?"

"You look for data that contradicts that story and for data that supports the story you want to tell yourself. Catherine, what's the story you'd like to tell yourself?"

Hmmm. I take a breath in, purse my lips, and slowly exhale. "Okay, fair enough. I am worthy of love and affection. I am capable of returning the same. There is space in my life to be both successful professionally and deeply connected with someone personally. There. That's it. That's the story I want to believe, that I need to believe, to move forward."

"Excellent, Catherine. Now, to gather data that supports this story. So, let's create two columns - data that supports the story you want to tell yourself and data that supports the story you have been telling yourself."

S is really a master. I wonder if her background includes psychology. She asks me questions and we agree on where the data goes on the chart. When we are finished, there are overwhelmingly more entries in the column supporting the story I want to tell myself. "Well, Catherine, I think the data supports the story you WANT to tell yourself, so start telling yourself that story." And with that the meeting is over.

I see Mas that night for a drink and dinner at his apartment. I debrief him on my meeting with S. He is clearly happy, jovial even. He holds my hand and just smiles. I find myself melting, my nipples becoming erect, and warmth gathering between my legs. He has staff remove the dishes and suggests we move to his study, that comfortable room off the front hall. He brings me a glass of sherry and we snuggle on the couch. I might as well be 16 years old at this moment. I am giddy, my heart beating rapidly. We kiss and talk and kiss and talk some more. He has me lie down, my head in his lap. We spend minutes just looking into each other's eyes. It is magical. I think to myself *another data point in the right column.* Our next sleepover isn't until the weekend. Our last embrace before I head home is intense. I can feel his erection pressing against my stomach. My hands find their way to his backside, one on each cheek. God, he has a nice ass.

Mas sees S on Thursday, but we don't reconnect until Saturday evening, this time at my place. I've planned only finger food -- sex food -- earthy and delicious but light enough to allow for energetic sex right after eating. There's sushi with caviar, sour cream, chopped green onion, and hard-boiled egg; a fruit plate with chocolate-dipped strawberries; mini-dark chocolate truffles for sweet; all accompanied by a Blanc de Noir champagne from Sonoma County. My assistant has given the staff the evening off and she waves good-bye once the food is in place. Amazing. My house without a crew of support staff.

Mas shares a bit about his meeting with S. Some things are to be a surprise. He would like to do at least one more round of scenes, each of us leading one, before the end of the month. He shares that there is something about going to the House of S that just heightens every experience. He proposes that he lead on the following Saturday. There is a twinkle in his eye while he waits for my reply. I make him wait a few seconds before I nod my assent.

Once we are upstairs, Mas asks if we can start in the shower. He carefully undresses me, taking time and care to wake up each zone as it becomes exposed. He nibbles on my shoulders, runs his fingertips up and down my neck, sucks on each nipple until it is raised and hard. He runs his hand inside my underwear before sliding them off. He pulls me close to kiss me and then drops to his knees. He sucks my clit into his mouth and moves his head so as to tug on it. Quickly, it is a solid sphere and cunt juice is starting to run down my legs. He pulls back to get a good look and says, "Good girl. Nicely warmed up. He stands and reaches around my back to spank my left cheek. "Your turn…"

Following his lead, I take my time removing his clothes. I make sure to lightly brush his crotch just enough to make him crazy. Before I remove his boxers, I liberate his cock, bending forward to take it into my mouth. I run my tongue in circles around the tip and then press down hard to take as much as possible into my mouth. Mas moans. I taste pre-cum and it is delicious. I slide his boxers down and take him by the hand to the shower.

There is some attempt at washing each other, but neither of us can stand the tension much longer. Mas lifts me up and puts my back against the tile wall. He presses his cock inside, but I say no, no, we need a condom. He runs soaking wet to get one, leaving footprints on the carpet. He returns, beaming, like he has the Golden Ticket, ripping the packet and unrolling the condom over a gleaming smooth erection. I am enthralled.

He bangs me hard, turning me around and bending me over. He holds my hips tightly and moves in and out, water streaming down at the juncture. We are both at the edge, but he slows down. "Not yet, Catherine. Not yet, my pet." He turns me around and holds my wrists pressing me again against the tile wall. His movement is slow and luscious. His mouth is all over me. I can't wait any longer. My back arches a bit and I press hard against his body. "That's my girl. I want to hear you cum." And I do. I cum so hard, I squirt. He is delighted. "Good girl. Let's get you dried off."

We move to the bed. He puts me on all fours and goes down between my legs from behind, running his tongue between my clit and perineum until I am once again a complete mess. He spys the coconut oil on the nightstand and slathers it all over the condom, making sure to coat the outside of my ass thoroughly. He presses slowly and my backside welcomes him. He is sliding in and out the full length of his cock. He uses his right hand to stroke my clit with a similar pattern. I cum long and hard and then I cum again. Finally, he allows himself to be carried away and the pulsing of cock in my ass is enough to send me once again into bliss. We collapse, still spooned together. Mas whispers, "You are becoming my precious pet."

We meet S together this time. It feels oddly comfortable, like we have been a couple forever. I catch myself thinking about the idea of being a couple. It feels good, right, somehow. I never thought I would say this. I feel my lips turn up a bit into a slight smile.

S, as always, has thoughtfully prepared for the meeting. There are adult drinks - very dry martinis in pre-chilled glasses, accompanied by prosciutto, melon, and a magnificent semi-hard cheese, a Manchego. An additional chair has been brought in and we are seated next to the window. This is the space S reserves for intimate conversations - tete a tete. Her assistant seats us and instructs us to relax and enjoy. S will be here any minute.

S does, indeed, arrive in a few minutes. She is regal, as always, in a flowing below the knee silk dress with elegant yet simple sandals, exposing well-maintained, attractive feet. Even the way she sits garners style points -- knees bent, ankles crossed, feet tucked to the right side.

"Mas, Catherine, so good to see you both. I trust you are well." We both smile and nod. "Excellent. Well, I sense that things are heating up between you, yes?" Mas and I look at each other and then back at S. We both assent, Mas tilting his head to the left and giving a slight nod, me tipping my chin down and back up. "So, I imagine you are wondering about next steps. I, too, have been giving this some thought, and I believe I have a solid plan." Mas reaches over and squeezes my hand. I am not used to public displays of affection, so this feels both awkward and lovely at the same time.

"It's important to realize that most people do not have a deep connection with their partners. What I am offering is a path to a level of connecting few ever experience. It takes work and thought, but really radical intimacy is about one's willingness to be fully open to another. My experience tells me that one way to open up emotionally and spiritually is to open up physically, perhaps in ways you've never known. My question to you both is, how willing are you to be vulnerable?" S pauses, hands gently folded in her lap. It's clear she is willing to let silence occupy whatever space is necessary for us to decide.

I notice I have shifted how I am sitting, moving to balance more on my left butt cheek. I realize this is AWAY from Mas. I catch myself and turn back to him, looking into his eyes with a hopeful gaze. "What do you think? Are we ready?" I realize Mas is speaking to me. It takes me a moment to process what he is saying. I want to reassure him that I am there, so I reach out and squeeze his hand.

I draw in a breath, look into his eyes and know this is it. If I say yes, I suspect we will be together for a long, long time. If I say no, I will return to the familiar and comfortable, the life I've lived up to this point. Is there really any choice? I smile and nod my head, "I am ready." To my surprise, I feel my heart leap in my chest. Catherine Standish Bolton -- ice queen, financier, feeling love.

Wow.

Shit, fuck, damn.

To cover the shock of the moment, I pick up my drink and take a sip. I realize this is my go-to, my way of covering my deepest feelings and desires -- being the successful, driven woman who created a respected house on Wall Street in what is most definitely still a man's world. What did I lose as a result? My humanity. Yes, my focus has served me well financially, but it has left me feeling hollow, living a life that feels like someone else's movie. It feels like I am stepping off a cliff. I find the courage to look into Mas's eyes for a moment. What I see melts my heart. He is looking at me with the most hopeful, gentle intention I can imagine. I smile back. He is perfect, and I now know this.

I take a deep breath in and turn to look at S. I can see she has deciphered what has transpired. She smiles gently at me and says, "I realize for both of you this shift requires a level of commitment you've not yet experienced. I can assure you, without reservation, that whatever happens will be transformative, but only if you step bravely forward. This is a matter of courage, not lust. How badly do you want to find out who you are at your most vulnerable? Most people sacrifice what's possible out of some misguided notion that they are protecting themselves. The truth is, only when opening up fully and completely will you ever experience who you truly are. So this is much more than just the possibility of a relationship between you -- this is an opportunity to find out who YOU each are, on your own." S again pauses to let all this sink in with an open but non-committal expression that simply communicates patience, patience for Mas and I to decide, patience to know if this is a place we are truly willing to go.

Blessedly, Mas speaks up, "S, Catherine and I are up for the challenge. We have developed a lovely connection, and I believe we both want to know where this can go. Right, Catherine?" Thankfully, Mas looks at me. Somehow I find the confidence I need in his eyes, his face open, expectant.

"Yes, absolutely. We are ready." And with that, we are off…

S explains that there will be a series of "assignments". We must faithfully follow the details of each. Assignments need to be completed during the week and on weekends. It will be an intense sequence. We both must commit to sticking with the schedule and making space in our lives for this to happen.

I squeeze Mas's hand and lean forward as if my proximity to Mas and to S will quiet my fluttering heart. Mas interprets my gesture as affirmation that all is well. I think to myself, *God, what have I done?*

Of course, S, ever the accurate reader of humans, must have sensed my hesitation and self-doubt. About an hour after I reached home, my assistant answered the door and brought in a small gift bag. Inside were a notecard with S's iconic initial and two enormous dark chocolate dipped strawberries.

> *Catherine,*
>
> *Every journey has key junctures, and you are certainly at one now. You have charted your own course with incredible success. It is natural and expected that embarking on a journey with someone will feel strange and unsettling. You might find yourself in flight, fight, or freeze mode, the telltale signs of which are not reaching out to Mas and/or finding excuses to cut short calls from him, creating a great excuse (likely related to a significant project at work) to delay this work for the foreseeable future, or even feeling irritable and*

looking for reasons to disagree with Mas (or me, for that matter) over small things. You are only human after all. And I invite you to look deeply inside yourself and ask, If not now, when? When will you embrace life in all its magnificent intensity, well beyond the adrenaline rush of mergers and acquisitions?

Your first exercise begins right now in this moment. Follow these instructions exactly as directed.

1. *Sit in a comfortable chair that isn't your "usual" chair.*
2. *Close your eyes.*
3. *Feel the texture of the chair with your hands, notice how it feels to sit in this comfortable but different chair.*
4. *Think about how you would describe the merits of this chair compared to your usual chair.*
5. *Open your eyes. Slowly eat the strawberries as though they are the last strawberries you will ever eat. Make the experience last. Take in the smell, the texture, the taste.*
6. *Write Mas a love note.*
7. *Sit in this new chair for the next 30 days. Do not sit in your usual chair.*

S.

That's it? Wow. Okay then. I muster the spirit to do the task. To my surprise, I struggle to define why the new chair isn't as good as the usual one, except that I *always* sit in the usual chair. When did I make THAT decision? Am I THAT habitual in my behavior?

I grab my laptop and write to Mas:

Sweet Mas,

I just ate the most amazing chocolate dipped strawberries. (S had instructed me to eat them very slowly as though they were the last ones I will ever eat.) I realized how many small things I simply miss. I never want it to be like that with you. I don't want to ever miss the small things. In the spirit of tuning into the small things, here's my top ten list of Mas's small things:

1. *You have the most amazing curve in your lower back.*
2. *Your skin is a luscious color and the texture is so smooth and flawless.*
3. *Your eyes speak to my soul. That's why I look at you when I need reassurance.*
4. *You listen to me. You don't simply wait for me to stop talking.*
5. *In the bedroom, you slow me down, make me wait, so the anticipation can build.*
6. *You take the lead in the most gentle way. It feels easy to follow.*
7. *You keep us focused on us and not the 900 business/market related things we could talk about.*
8. *Your legs...seriously, your legs.*
9. *The way you position me -- up against a wall, on all fours, on my back -- I feel like a flexible doll with the most capable handler.*
10. *How your tongue feels on my clit. More specifically, how you get a hold of it and make small circles with your mouth. This transports me to other realms!*

Honestly, the list could go on and on. I just want you to know I see the countless lovely small things, and you are more than the sum of all of them.

- Catherine

I click *"send"* and close my eyes, imagining how he will react on reading my love letter. Then, I realize something far more extraordinary: this is the first love letter I have ever written.

The next assignment comes via email the following day.

Catherine and Mas,
Your next assignment is to meet at the Carriage Hotel tonight. I have arranged a room and catering. Bring only the clothing you need to wear the next day. Instructions will be in the room. These will be specific and I expect you both to adhere to them.

S.

Mas messages me that he would like to pick me up and should he come to the office or my home. I decide it will be easier to leave straight from work. I want as much time as possible with him.

We arrive and the hotel clerk states the classic phrase, "Welcome. We've been expecting you," nonchalantly. We take the key and assure him that we can manage our bags. Mas, very sweetly, takes mine as well as his.

The room is palatial with silk paneled walls, a magnificent chandelier, and the most impressive canopied bed. There's a fireplace already lit and glowing. A table holds a champagne bucket with a bottle of Louis Roederer Cristal, a ridiculously delicious and expensive champagne. There are those same dark chocolate dipped strawberries, brie and seeded crackers, and red pear slices. A card on the table has the number 1 on it.

"Mas, should we open this," I ask, holding up the card. He nods. I slide out the cardstock insert and immediately recognize S's handwriting.

Happy honeymoon! And like all great honeymoons, you will spend tonight exploring each other, slowly, seductively.

Begin by undressing each other. You may caress, touch, and kiss, but no sex acts.

Slide into the silk robes and then come to the table and enjoy the champagne and nibbles while reading card 2.

S

Wow. I am speechless and a bit wide-eyed. I look up and Mas is looking at me with his reassuring eyes. "Catherine, let's be faithful to the instructions, okay? If S has planned it, this will surely be amazing, a night to remember, our first honeymoon." My heart skips a beat hearing these last three words.

The undressing part is a test of will. Mas takes the lead and has me sit in a chair while he slips off my shoes. I've come from the office, so I am wearing hose. I decided at the last minute to wear a garter belt, a really lovely one I'd bought years ago from a boutique in San Francisco between the Mission District and Japantown. Mas runs the back of his hand slowly up the inside of my leg till it touches a garter. He pauses and his eyes widen on the discovery. He slowly runs three fingers back down to my feet.
There's an ottoman nearby, and he stops to pull it over. He gently grabs my arms, helping me slide back deeply into the chair, then he lifts my legs with one hand and moves the ottoman into place with the other. I notice how graceful he is, each movement effortless. I feel my legs being lowered onto the ottoman.

Mas kneels to the side and begins to stroke my legs again. He varies the pressure at times, but the pace is slow, seductive, and dreamy. I feel myself relaxing, my eyes closing, and yes, my cunt getting wet.

After some time, Mas reaches up under my dress with both hands and undoes a garter. He does this with the same ease and grace as before. I wonder how many garters he has unclipped. He allows his fingers to stray just a bit, brushing the tips ever so slightly against my crotch. My cunt juice has begun to soak my silk panties, and he feels this. He looks at me and smiles wryly, "What a good girl you are, Catherine. What a good girl."

This tantalizing and excruciatingly slow process continues until he has slipped off both stockings. I think he is going to move onto other areas, but he lingers, kissing my legs and moving closer and closer to my crotch. He stops right before he gets there. Taking in a deep breath with his nose, he closes his eyes, and his face tilts back, and as he breathes out, he lowers his chin and I find myself again looking straight into those eyes. "Catherine, I love how you smell."

He begins to slide my dress up. I lift one cheek and then the other till my dress is gathered around my waist. Mas sits back and just looks at me for a moment. "God, you are so fucking gorgeous."

He slides my panties down, reaching around and underneath my ass. I lift my hips a bit and he presses his hands against my cheeks in the most sensual way. A slight moan leaves my lips. He moves his hands to the front and pulls my panties down, but not without first teasing me with seemingly casual brushing of the pubic bone. Again he breathes in my scent. "Oh, my, Catherine. I think I should get a towel for you to sit on. I don't want to share any of your luscious scent with anyone else, housekeeper or future guest." I feel myself blush. I am totally turned on, cunt juice now oozes freely and I can do nothing to stop it.

It takes at least 30 minutes for Mas to get all my clothes off. I truly have no sense of time. I am in a kind of trance state, highly aroused but not moving toward any kind of climax. It is both maddening and delicious.

He brings the silk robe and has me stand to put it on. He attends to every detail (another thing I love about him), including tying the belt just so. He looks down at me and then pulls me into his arms, kissing me with unhurried passion.

I feel his erection pressing against my stomach. The cunt juice begins to run down my inner thighs. But it's my time to undress him and I choose a different approach altogether…

I push myself away just enough so I can unbutton his shirt. I leave the last two buttons fastened. I begin to slide the shirt off his shoulders slowly but then I tug hard so the shirt is now halfway down and pinning his arms just a bit. I push myself away from him, admiring the casual bondage effect. I leave him standing and walk around him till I am behind. I cup his cheeks like I am checking the quality of a specimen. I slide my arms around and unfasten his belt. Unzipping his fly, I let my wrists and palms press ever so slightly against his erection. I feel a wet spot where his pre-cum has soaked through his briefs. I work his trousers down just far enough where they fall to his ankles. Mas starts to step out of them. I slap his right buttock hard, "Not, yet, my love. This is my dance."

I realize how much I love having him in this rather vulnerable spot. I imagine what it might be like to actually secure his ankles and wrists together and my cunt responds, more pearlesque liquid working its way down my legs.

I continue my circumnavigation and return to face him. I grab his t-shirt up by his neck with both hands and pull in opposite directions, the visual of his emerging chest joins the pleasing sound of tearing fabric. I pause and look up. Mas's eyes have widened a bit, a mix of curiosity and surprise. My mouth finds his left nipple and I suck on it hard, working it into an erect cylinder. Pulling away just slightly, I blow on it. The cylinder grows more erect still. I love feeling his body respond to me like this. To show him how pleased I am, I hold his gaze while guiding the back of his left thumb to just below my cunt where it is now slippery and wet. His eyes widen further. I bend down and lick the juice off his hand. The bulge in his briefs grows.

I slip my thumbs under the elastic waist of his briefs. I slowly move my hands around to lift them away from his skin, shimmying them down in centimeter increments. His erection looks ridiculous at this point, pressing hard against the fabric tent that I am not yet willing to liberate. I feel his butt tighten. I grab both checks and press against him hard. He moans.

I kneel down so my face is level with his cock as I finally lift the waistband up and over his erection. He is looking down, my mouth just inches away, as I turn my cheek, casually brushing against him. He moans again. I help him step out of his pants and briefs. Before I stand, I run my hands around to his backside, pressing his cheeks apart and pulling his pelvic bone toward my face. He is dying.

I make him stand waiting with his arms still lightly pinned by his shirt as I get his robe. The sight of him naked, cock fully erect, and arms pinned makes me absolutely crazy. I refuse to let on. I continue my slow, delicious torture as I help him out of his shirt and into the robe, his erection still standing forth as I tie the bow of the robe's belt. I make sure and give it a gentle pat, knowing full well it is seeking more, much, much more.

We sit at the table where a chilled bottle of Veuve Clicquot Brut Rose rests up to its neck in an ice water bath. Art nouveau flutes with vined stems adjacent on a linen covered tray. Petit four, sugar coated almonds, melon bites wrapped in prosciutto, truffle black pepper cream cheese spread on seeded nut bread topped with bits of prune, stuffed green olives baked in cheese pastry. It is a luscious sight. However luscious, there is only one thing Mas and I are thinking about. Still, we follow S's lead and open the envelope marked #2.

Waiting...wanting...and waiting some more - this is what makes things sweet. So, you will set the timer on the table for 30 minutes. You will sip, nibble, flirt with no actual contact. Then and only then may you read card #3, resting on the bed.

S

Mas sighs and smiles at me. He opens the champagne and we toast...to us, to the evening, to where things take us. I am surprised that I am able to taste the food. I decide to feed Mas a nibble as a way to flirt. I pick up a melon ball, and bending and reaching across, make sure my robe falls open enough for him to see my breasts. His eyes widen a bit and twinkle at me. He takes his time pulling the melon and ham off the toothpick. He reciprocates, feeding me a gorgeous petit four with pink icing covering chocolate cake, topped with a crystalized violet. I swear I can smell the violet and memories of my childhood picking a bundle of violets from a neighbor's shade garden to present to my mother pops up in my head. We sip, feed each other, our bodies and faces telling a story that words cannot do justice to. This dance continues till the chime on the timer goes off. I realize how quickly 30 minutes has passed.

Mas says, "Shall we?" We stand and move to the bed where note #3 is propped up against a pile of pillows. He opens it and reads:

You will flip the enclosed coin to determine who will lead tonight. You both have shown the ability to dominate and submit, so it seems only appropriate to let chance decide who is calling the shots tonight. Bon chance to each of you.

S

Oh, my. Interesting. Mas picks up the coin and asks me to call it. I choose tails. And the coin the lands...heads.

Mas's eyes widen. There is something wild lurking behind his gentleness, a boldness coming to the fore. I breathe in. Here we go.

Mas takes me by the shoulders and turns me around, pushing me face down onto the bed. With one hand pressing between my shoulder blades to signal me to stay put, he runs his other hand up my thigh to my crotch. He does this a few times and in my impatience I wiggle. My movement is met with a hard spank to my butt and stern admonishment to hold still. He begins again. I am growing wetter by the minute. Finally, after what seems like an eternity, he runs his hand from my public bone to my cunt. He thrusts two fingers inside and I gasp, not from the action but from the dramatic change in tempo. He gathers up some slippery secretions and slathers this onto my clit. I gasp again. My clit was already erect. It is now throbbing. His fingers dive back into my cunt and then out to spread more cunt juice, this time on my ass. He tells me to hold still.

I hear the sound of a condom wrapper tearing, and then his cock pressing against my ass. He wraps his right hand around to massage my clit and he presses the head inside my ass. I moan as the sensation is both painful and pleasurable. He slows a bit, letting my ass relax before moving in and out, ever more deeply. He now has both hands wrapped around me working my clit. One hand pulls upward to move the hood that covers the it. Now exposed, the sensation of his other hand relentlessly rubbing it is almost too much. But Mas doesn't speed up. If anything, as I get close to cumming, he slows down. It is nearly unbearable, this dance to the edge and back, over and over.

His left hand reaches up to grab my hair at the roots. He pulls my head up and increases his tempo. He tells me, "Look at me. Look at me while I fuck you. Look at me when you cum. I need to see your eyes." I turn my head, glad for the connection. I curl my left arm under my head and stare directly into his eyes. He lets the tempo build, punctuating some deep thrusts with more frantic pressure on my clit. I feel myself rising higher and higher, and then there it is. I am cumming.

"I am cumming, Mas, I am cumming. Please don't stop. Fuck me. Fuck me hard." And he does. He holds me in a space, a delicious, time-suspended space, and my orgasm just builds and builds. I am crying out to God, Jesus, and Mas. Finally, I reach a place of explosive sensation and he lets himself go, the spasming of his cock in my ass prolonging my orgasm even more. He collapses on top of me, his cock still inside.

"Catherine, you are so fucking good. God, you are so fucking good. What a good girl you are, my pet. And you are my pet. Mine."

I consider these words. His. I am his. Have I ever truly belonged to anyone? I am not sure, but I am certain I belong to him. No one has ever made me feel this way. The connection I had with Adam was eye-opening but the one I have with Mas is beyond words. It is becoming something, something meaningful, tantalizing, not like anything I have ever known.

Mas pulls out and takes me by the hand, leading me into the bathroom. He sits me down at the vanity while he removes the condom and starts the bath. "Catherine, may I wash your lovely body? I want to feel your curves with slippery, soapy hands." I nod and head to the commode to pee. I turn to sit and there stands Mas, preventing me from closing the door. "My love, I need to taste you, all of you." He sits me down and kneels before me, extending a hand between my thighs. "Please, Catherine, I need to taste your piss. I need to know all of you." I exhale, close my eyes, and let the urine flow. My clit is still swollen. As the urine presses past it, the sensation builds and I orgasm. I open my eyes. Mas is licking his fingers, smiling sweetly. "Catherine, you are a delight. How blessed I am to call you mine." He leaves me to tend to the bath.

I wake the next morning with Mas holding me close. He stirs and I feel an erection building. I smile, recalling last night's intense fuck. He asks me if I think the coin thing is still in play. I say sure, why not. And with that, he rolls me over and fucks me like a teenager, little to no foreplay, hot and heavy to get going, a complete 180 from last night and still incredible, sexy, hot. He controls himself enough to allow me to cum several times before he explodes. Mas is nothing if not considerate, I think.

We eat a reasonable breakfast, chased by well-made coffee Americano. I note that Mas also adds nothing to his coffee. (I have long believed that adulterating the brew is a sin quite unlike all others!) After check out, we kiss on the cheek and head to our prospective offices. I try to process my feelings. I am so comfortable with him and yet also very intrigued. There is enough mystery to keep me wanting more and enough comfort to allow me to relax and fully be me. I pause to consider if I have ever felt this way about anyone. Have I ever been in a place where I can truly be me? I decide to arrange a meeting with S. It feels like an important juncture is at hand and I need her guidance.

Always gracious, S greets me warmly and invites me to nestle into one of the comfy chairs near the window. She has chosen an interesting mix of drink and food, quite unlike what she has offered so far. There is Heradura Gold Tequila, lime wedges, and salt. Bottles of Corona beer float in an ice water bath. Tortilla chips, toasted with gooey cheese and topped with a slice of jalapeno rest on a brightly painted plate. A bowl of corn and onion salsa, as well as a green salsa -- tomatillo perhaps? -- complete the offerings.

S sits down. She looks rather casual in khaki slacks and a form fitting t-shirt with a cheeky scarf around her neck. I realize her attire matches the food and drink. Damn, she is perfect.

An assistant enters with chilled beer glasses and pours tequila shots (four of them!) and fills the glasses with iced Corona. S dips a lime wedge in the salt and raises a shot glass. I follow suit. I mimic her actions to the t -- chug the shot and then bite down hard on the salted lime wedge. Chase the shot with a significant quantity of beer. Smile. Eat several chips, alternating salsa offerings.

S pauses long enough to smile. "Catherine, I hope you realize where you are in your journey. I wonder if you are even aware of your growth."

I smile back, take in a breath, and respond, "S, I am in a new place, one I have never been in before. That's why I requested this meeting."

She meets my gaze and tilts her head slightly. I take this as encouragement to continue.

"So, as you know, I have been really focused on building Bolton Financial. Every ounce of energy has gone to this. I realized some months back that this achievement, building a large successful enterprise as a woman operating very much in a man's world, had cost me a lot. I make a fantastic living at the cost of having a life. I came to you to reconnect, to begin to live again. I feel I certainly am living now. My life is rich in experience and connection. Perhaps more importantly, I have learned to fully let go. I don't think I knew how to do this before."

"It was easy with Adam. I always understood he was not truly mine. Regardless of how close I grew to him, I knew he and I were not going to live happily ever after. Then you introduced me to Mas. Well, this is where I feel I need your counsel."

S raises her right eyebrow slightly. I pause to collect my thoughts. Before I continue, she interrupts, "Are you falling in love, Catherine?"

"S, this is what I am asking myself. Honestly, I don't even know what falling in love is."

"Catherine, falling in love has much more to do with being genuine and vulnerable to another more than with anything else. It hinges on one's willingness to be intimate, radically intimate. Many people think they are in love when in fact they are simply in lust. Mind you, lust is not a bad thing, but lust can be satisfied. Love, on the other hand, generates an endless hunger that is only satisfied by one's lover. So, perhaps the question you might need to ask yourself is do you feel a hunger, one that will never be fully satisfied, with Mas?"

Before I can respond, Catherine raises another shot glass. Her facial expressions indicate I am to follow suit. I dip my lime wedge in the salt and tip my head back as the smooth yet fiery tequila hits the back of my throat. The tart lime is the relief I need from the post-shot burn. And then the cold Corona chaser softens the blow. I stop to enjoy a few chips, dipping them in the tomatillo salsa.

"S, here's what I know. He is exciting. He is smart. He can hold his own with me." And with that sentence I stop cold. I realize the import of this. Mas can, indeed, hold his own with me. Others may have tried in the past, but Mas has been the only one I have willingly bowed down to. What made that submission so effortless?

"You are discovering that there is joy in letting go. There is beauty in giving up one's power to another. It is the beauty of receiving. How does it feel to be the object of someone's desire? How does it feel to give that person free rein over your body?"

Receiving. Desire. Free rein. Yes, but there is a nagging wondering emerging. "S, the other day when Mas and I were at the hotel, it was my turn to undress him. I pulled his shirt down so that it pinned his arms. I left him with his feet in his slacks. I toyed with the waistband of his underwear. And I was completely aroused by this. But these actions are not submissive in the least. What does this mean?"

"Catherine, you and Mas are both quite dominant in your day-to-day lives. For one to have balance, both of you should, at times, be submissive. It is not only okay it is important for you to feel this from time-to-time. Because you are the owner of a large and successful Wall Street firm and Mas works for one, you should seek submission more than he does. This is simply because that is what you need for balance."

"You have always been the one in control. And if not in control, you have taken control over. This is your natural state, but it is not a balanced one. Submit to Mas and find your balance. And, when circumstances allow, give him the same opportunity."

And with those words, I sensed our meeting was at an end. S smiled and promised the next task would help me sort things out. I swallowed the last of my beer, washing down another yummy chip, and smiled back. I trusted her. She had brought me this far. She would carry me to the end.

When I reached home, there was a basket and a note. How does she do this? Inside the basket was a pint of Herradura with a simple note, "For when your courage lags…" And, of course, a lovely handwritten card:

Catherine,

Radical intimacy is to reveal oneself completely without reservation. The next tasks will demand this of you. Know that however hard these are, you are ready for whatever you encounter. Remember, this is a journey to know yourself above all else."

S

Hmmm, ever the enigma, S has definitely raised my curiosity. I will know soon enough. Our next task is the coming weekend. I find myself struggling to concentrate even at work. My mind keeps wandering to flashes of images from last weekend -- Mas fucking me in the ass, Mas undressing me painfully slowly, Mas fucking me like a teenager. Me undressing Mas. Especially this...Mas rather helpless, mildly restrained, subject to me.

My instructions arrive on Friday. They are simple, to the point. I find myself excited and somewhat terrified:

Find your courage, Catherine. This weekend will start with you very much in control and will end with you very much subject to Mas's control. It's time to experience the full spectrum of what's possible.

S

We meet at a very hip boutique hotel. The front desk clerk hands over a card that tells us to relax in the bar over a drink. I am wearing a red leather skirt, an impulse buy that I've never had the courage to wear before, and a white button-down shirt. Over the shirt is a striking but simple red harness. Mas is clearly pleased, "Catherine, you are fucking stunning." I smile inwardly and outwardly. I love the attention.

He orders a dry martini. I order a Bellini and then change my mind: a shot of the best tequila the house has and a Corona chaser. The waiter grins. This girl means business.

When the drinks arrive, Mas watches as I knock back the shot and bite down hard on the salted lime wedge. I drink the Corona straight from the bottle. I am feeling raw, powerful. The tequila has a fortifying effect. I cannot wait to make love to Mas on my terms.

When we reach the room, I restrain myself from grabbing S's note that rests on the dresser. Mas opens it and then hands it to me:

Tonight and tomorrow are all about flexing between dominance and submission. Be prepared to explore as a receiver and a giver. Catherine, you are up first…

S

Oh, my. I have fantasized about this day, but suddenly feel anything but ready. Then the image of Mas mildly restrained flashes through my head and I feel heat growing between my legs. I let my cunt call the shots. Whatever she wants, this is what I will do.

I walk over to where Mas is standing. He sees my sly smile and reacts with a rather shy one back. Good. He is already moving toward submission. This is where I need him to be. I run my fingers over his chest and around to his back. I make sure he feels my penetrating gaze. I want him to feel like an object of desire, owned by me. I take his chin in my hand and move his head side to side, inspecting his face. I hear myself saying, "You, my pet, are gorgeous. Today, you will please me greatly." Blood rushes to his face. He is blushing. He is feeling his place. It is lovely to behold.

I unbutton his trousers, brushing my hand against his cock. It responds, pressing back against my hand. I drop his trousers to his ankles. He starts to step out of them and I slap his ass hard. "You are to do as you are told. Do you understand?" His eyes widen. He nods and drops his gaze. "That's a good boy. You know what's expected." His cock reveals his true response. It is now pressing against his briefs hard.

I realize my body is also responding, my panties barely able to hold the moisture oozing from my cunt. My labia are swelling and my ass is begging for fingers, his cock, a toy.

I play with the waistband of his briefs, letting the elastic snap back against his skin to where he jumps slightly. I ease them down, lifting the front over his swollen cock. When they drop to his ankles, I stand back. His shirt tails hang down but his cock is protruding. I circle around to the back. I press up against him, squeezing each cheek with one hand and then spank each hard. My hand is burning and his skin is reddening. His cock stands up a bit more.
From the back, I slide my right hand around to caress his balls. He moans. My left hand is gently moving out and in over his cock. Pre-cum is oozing freely.

I unbutton the first four buttons of his shirt. I pull it down rather roughly so that it is gathered at his waist, not exactly pinning his arms, but restraining their use. I trace my fingers across his chest. He moans again. *Not yet, my pet. Not yet.*

I come back around to the front and begin an assault on his nipples. I am merciless. I am sucking, pulling, and sucking some more. I blow on them. I watch them pucker and extend. I work them until they are beautiful erect cylinders. Mas starts to move against me. I won't tolerate that. I smack his ass hard. "You are to do as I direct. Is that understood?" Mas nods again, his chin dropping lower.

I drop to my knees, facing his now ridiculously erect cock. I take only the glans into my mouth. In and out. In and out. In and out. I pull my mouth off and look at pre-cum dribbling out. He is hungry, very hungry.

I instruct him to step out of his trousers and come to the bed. I turn him away and push him forward. He is now chest down, butt in the air, arms still pinned lightly to his side. I spread his cheeks and dive in with my mouth. Animal sounds come from him. I am licking, pressing my tongue against his ass. I am moving from perineum to ass and back. I am caressing his balls. His dick craves my touch but I am ignoring it. Pre-cum is dripping off his cock now.

I instruct him to stay right where he is, ass in the air. I head to the bathroom and put on a harness with a rather large dildo. I pull my skirt over it and return, carrying a container of coconut oil.

I dip my hand into the creamy liquid and massage it into Mas's ass, my fingers pressing and moving in and out ever so slightly, first one finger, then two, then three. He is moaning uncontrollably now. I am relentless. I tell him, "I want you to look at me when I fuck you. Look at me." He turns his head as I pull up my skirt, revealing the dildo. His eyes widen as he watches me slather coconut oil up and down the shaft. I grab his shirt with one hand and with the other, begin pressing the dildo into his ass. He is moaning. His cock is more erect than ever. I am patient but merciless.

As he opens up and the dildo begins to move in and out, I move my right hand to his cock. The coconut oil lets me slide up and down the shaft in timing with my movement in his ass. He is dying, moaning, drooling, begging with unintelligible words. I simply continue the assault. He cums in massive spasms. I catch much of the cum in my hand. When he is done, I pull out from his ass slowly. I roll him over and begin to feed him his cum. I share in the repast, tasting the salty sticky sweetness that is him.

I let him rest. I consider removing the harness and dildo but decide it is better for him to feel submissive if he feels the dildo up against his butt cheeks and pressing between his legs. I hike up my skirt and spoon him, making sure the dildo is noticeable. He doesn't fight this. Instead, he closes his eyes, his muscles relax, and his breathing eases. How beautiful that he let me dominate him. How easily he slipped into a submissive state. He is remarkable.

When I am sure he is asleep, I slip away to fetch a special toy, something I have wanted to try. It's made of stainless steel and looks like a small egg on a slightly curved shaft. It's a prostate massager. The dildo has opened him up. Now I want to remove his control and massage the semen out of his prostate ducts. He won't be able to control this. His milk will simply flow.

He begins to stir. I offer water and a warm smile. Then I hold up the device. His eyes flash. I pat his behind gently. "My love, you will give in to me as I have given in to you. I will be gentle, but you will give in to me." He nods.

I begin by massaging his butt cheeks with long, luscious strokes. He is relaxing again. I move closer to his anus and with a well-oiled hand move from the back of his balls to his tailbone and back again, over and over. His ass begins to relax. I slide a finger in and out. He is moaning and his cock is stirring. I insert a lube injector preloaded with coconut oil and press the plunger. Next, I circle his ass with the metal egg. I have warmed it between my legs. His anus seems eager to accept it, so I slide it in. Mas moans louder. He can feel the fullness in his rectum as I move the egg up to his prostate and begin a series of come-hither movements the device is engineered to produce.

Initially, he just moans with each stroke. His cock is becoming more and more erect. And then, one stroke produces a spurt of semen dribbling from the head of his penis. The next stroke, the same. On and on I go, Mas moaning, eyes rolled back, mouth open, his cock leaking white milk in copious quantities. His erection grows. I move one hand over and begin stroking it. Now he is in a primal state, his prostate milk flowing, his balls engaged in releasing sperm. His moans turn guttural. I pick up the rhythm and very quickly he cums hard, his whole body shaking in one massive release.

I feel the power of his submission. I am in control of his body and he has allowed this. It is amazing. It doesn't matter that I haven't had an orgasm. It doesn't matter that I am not sexually stimulated. What matters is the pleasure and release I have given him and he has allowed.

Slowly, I remove the prostate massager. I roll Mas onto his back and cover him sweetly with a blanket. I stroke his head. I tell him how amazing he is. How much I love bringing him pleasure. What a good boy he was to let me tend to him.

He drifts off again. I tend to washing up the toys and getting undressed. This is all for tonight. Tomorrow is his day. I cannot wait.

I snuggle in next to him. He rolls over and presses his sticky crotch against my ass. The sensation of the cum brings back the sensation of control. It was amazing to manipulate his body so.

We wake up around 8, quite late for two finance types. I draw a bath and dump in the full container of bubble bath. The scent of ylang ylang fills the air. Mas is standing and peeing. I cuddle up behind him, reaching around to hold his cock. He allows this and I feel the stream of piss moving through his cock. I am not certain what to do when the stream stops. He takes over and I slide around to the front, offering my mouth. He smiles and shakes a few drops of piss into it. Slightly bitter with a hint of salt. This is Mas in the morning, I think.

I take a turn while he watches. It feels intimate, not prying. I think about this. Months ago this would have been the strangest experience. Now it just feels sweet and close.

We slide into the tub. I lay back against his chest. His hands reach around to my crotch. "Catherine, my sweet, I didn't mean to ignore you last night. I promise I will take good care of you today." He grabs my clit and gives it a little pinch, and like that, it starts to swell.

We eat breakfast in the room, snuggled in terry cloth robes. I decide to be brave. "Mas, did you enjoy last night?"

He pauses, then replies. "Catherine, that was the most amazing sexual experience I have ever had, and perhaps not for the obvious reasons." He takes a sip of coffee. I stay mute, hoping he will elaborate. "I cannot think of a time when I wasn't focused on my partner's pleasure. Believe me, I enjoy giving you pleasure, I do. But I have never simply had pleasure given to me. And the fact that you made that possible by clearly taking control was amazing as well. I know how powerful you are. Everyone on the street knows how powerful you are. It was lovely to be brought to such heights of pleasure by your power."

I think about this for a moment -- power as a means of bringing pleasure. This puts so much into perspective. Submission can be a dream-state because one relinquishes control. One slides into a place where another takes over, serving deeply and completely. It felt so good to give so much pleasure to Mas, to watch his body shake and convulse, to hear animal sounds leave his throat, to see him exhausted, spent, vulnerable. He trusts me. He trusts me that I will care for him. He trusts that my focus is on him.

After breakfast, Mas smiles and says simply, "My turn." I feel a chill of anticipation. "Catherine, take off your robe and lie face down on the bed."

I do as I am told. I feel myself sliding ever so gently into submission.

Mas is going through his suitcase. He returns. He slides a blindfold over my eyes. He secures my wrists together over my head. He tethers my ankles to each other, and then he slides a ball into my mouth. I realize he is gagging me. Oh my. This is something new. Even Adam allowed me to have a voice.

Mas begins to run his fingers over my body. I warm to the sensation. His touch is light and slow. He dances ever so close to erogenous zones. My body responds, relaxes, moisture releasing between my legs. There is a pause. My attention strains to make sense of sounds but he is very quiet. Suddenly, I feel a dozen stings on my ass. He is flogging me. The tempo and intensity are manageable. He is hanging right at the edge of what I can withstand. It's the pause between each blow that keeps the tears back. I begin to drool onto the pillow.

Mas pauses to stroke my red ass. The touch feels painful but also comforting. He begins again. Blow after blow. The sensation is moving from pain to numbness. I am grateful for this. He stops again. My skin craves the sensation now. I want him to continue but am powerless to say so. Of his own accord, he continues. Suddenly he stops and puts his hand into my crotch. He spreads my labia and explores the edges of my cunt, now smooth and slippery with secretions. He pulls my hips up and shoves pillows under them. I feel the mattress move. Perhaps he is on the bed? Then I feel his hands spreading my cheeks. He starts licking my cunt. I crave penetration but he is taking his time. He moves to my ass, circling the edges of my anus and then pressing against it forcefully. I am making sounds, audible and unintelligible. He moves fingers in and out of my cunt while his tongue torments my ass. I am dying.

There is a pause, then the sensation of coconut oil being slathered on my ass. He slides in a toy, a medium-sized plug. I feel my body relax and take it in. The feeling of fullness is a relief. Mas rolls me over and again puts pillows under my hips. I hear the sound of a wrapper tearing. Then, thankfully, blessedly, his cock thrusting into my cunt.

It is tight, the plug narrowing the neck significantly. The angle of penetration pushes his cock against my g-spot. Oh, my, this IS good. Fuck. So good. Drool is running down my cheek and I don't fucking care. I am focused on the sensation. It is over the top. I cum hard. My cunt now wetter than ever, he continues pushing, in and out, hard, deep, pressing my g-spot. His hand finds my clit and moves in diagonals, pressing against my pubic bone. I feel sensation rising in my feet, moving up my legs, and then rising in my clit and my cunt at the same time. Jesus. I cannot cry out. Only muffled moans and sounds of increasing intensity come out. Mas holds me in this space for what seems like minutes. I am a fountain of sensation that feels endless. Finally, there is a powerful contraction, followed by several others. I feel a pool of wetness beneath. My god, I have squirted.

Mas still hasn't cum, so he only slows his movements just enough for me to begin to recover. Moments later he is again rubbing my clit with his thumb and fucking me hard. Shit. Fuck. Damn. I hear sloshing sounds out of my wet cunt. I feel the energy again rising. Holy fuck. I cum again. He somehow holds me in that space right at the edge. Me, moaning, head moving side to side. Unbelievable pleasure in my body as the kundalini builds and builds then fountains up my spine and out my head. Holy fuck. A tantric orgasm. Shit. I have only read about these.

As drools pours over my cheek, Mas increases his speed, cumming hard. The narrowed space from the plug pressing up toward my vagina allows me to feel the spasms of his cock in glorious detail. I wish I could smile but the gag prevents this. He grunts and presses hard in one final gasp. It is in this moment that I think, I want to bear this man's children.

I blush at the idea. Crazy notion. Primal instinct. Still…

The day is a blur. Mas is relentless. My orgasms seemingly infinite, but also intense. The more I cum, the more determined he is to make me cum. He (thankfully) removes the gag after the first round. The blindfold, some rounds later. The restraints, even later. By that time, I am incapable of self-propelled movement. Shit. I am unaware of time, space, or even the separation between him and me.

Finally, he stops. He tends to me in the most loving way. He runs a bath. He carries me to the toilet and holds me upright so I can pee. He then carries me to the tub, sliding me into the water. He joins and supports my body with his. Apparently, he called housekeeping and requested clean sheets because after he wraps me in a bath sheet and carries me back, the bed is crisp and freshly made. He props me up with pillows and insists that I drink weak tea and orange juice. He feeds me bites of sandwich with his hands. He slips a Jordan almond into my mouth and admonishes me to rub my tongue against the sugar coating. Soon enough, I am returning to the world.

After he is certain I am returning to full consciousness, he lays beside me, stroking my hair. "Catherine, I love you." I realize what he has just said. He says it again, "Catherine, I love you and I want you." My heart leaps. "Catherine, I want us to be together. What do you say?"

Quickly he adds, "Oh, sweetheart. Let me let you recover. How unthoughtful of me. I am just so over the moon for you. You are perfect for me. You let me experience the full range of who I am. I have never met anyone quite like you before, and I want to be with you, if you will have me."

He goes to the phone and orders drinks and dinner. He helps me into my robe. I am still feeling like jello. He gets me into a very comfortable chair and props my feet up onto the ottoman. He rubs them so very sweetly while we wait for dinner. He speaks gently and softly. I am more aware of the tone than the content, still very much in my subspace, my dream-state, seemingly unable to leave just yet.

He takes a throw from the other chair and lays it over my lap. He is attentive, loving, kind. I ask myself, what have I done to deserve this person, this lovely human? The buzzer rings and a waiter brings in dinner. It smells yummy, but I cannot even move my arms. Mas realizes this and alternates feeding me and himself. Sips of gin and tonic, bites of steak, mashed potatoes, and tender green beans. The food tastes amazing, like it's from another planet. I am grateful he is feeding me. I chew, swallow, and smile in endless cycles. Finally, I manage a sentence, "Mas, what did I do to deserve you?"

"Oh, my pet. This is what I ask myself daily. You and I, we were meant for each other. How could we even explain to anyone our connection, how deep and intimate it is? But there it is. Real. True. Beautiful. I know we need to nurture this, and I may have been premature in confessing my love for you, but there it is."

"May I have some time to make sense of this? Please don't see this as anything but my need to come to a place on my own. Do you understand?"

"Catherine, I will wait for you. I worship you. You are my life, and I will wait for however long it may take."

I close my eyes and drift off. I awaken in the wee hours of the night. Mas has managed to tuck me into bed. He is holding me, our feet touching. My hand is on his cock. He is breathing evenly into my ear. I am at peace, perhaps for the first time in my adult life.

I realize that I have aways to go to understand what commitment to love means, but I am certain I will figure this out. I feel a wave of gratitude that I have Mas to help me get there. And, of course, S. No doubt her guidance and direction will help me on my journey.

So where am I now? I have rediscovered true bliss in both giving and receiving unconditionally. I have found pleasure in pain and pain in pleasure. I am seeing myself as a whole human being. This is enough. I am living again. I am able to be completely in the now, in the drea-state that suspends time. And I can give this gift to someone else. In that sense, my journey, while continuing, is complete.

Made in the USA
Columbia, SC
27 June 2024

5d47d964-9d68-4f04-8ec1-531347a2bed2R01